CW00833706

THE NEW MOSCOW PHILOSOPHY

Vyacheslav Pyetsukh

THE NEW MOSCOW PHILOSOPHY

translated from the Russian by Krystyna Anna Steiger

TWISTED SPOON PRESS • PRAGUE • 2011

ISBN 978-80-86264-36-3

PRINCIPAL CHARACTERS

Belotsvetov, Nikita Ivanovich: pharmacologist

Chinarikov, Vasily (Vasia, Vaska): the caretaker and resident philosopher

Fondervyakin, Lev Borisovich (Lyova): preserved fruit enthusiast

Golova, Yulia (Yulka): divorced mother

Lyubov (Lyuba) and Pyotr (Petka, Pet): Golova's children

Kapitonova, Anna Olegovna: grandmother

Nachalov, Dmitry (Dima, Mitya, Mitka): Kapitonova's grandson

Pumpianskaya, Alexandra Sergeyevna: the old lady

Rybkin: the district inspector

Valenchik, Genrikh Ivanovich: aspiring writer

Valenchik, Vera Alexandrovna: the pregnant wife

Vanya: the locksmith

Vostryakova: the building superintendent

FRIDAY

1

It's astonishing, but from time immemorial the Russian sense of self has been under the dominion, even the yoke, of its native discourse. The Danes didn't read their Kierkegaard for a hundred years, the French didn't take orders from Stendhal until he was pushing up daisies, while in this country some school teacher from Saratov — the son of a priest — writes that for the sake of the nation's future it'd be good to learn to sleep on a bed of nails, and half the nation starts sleeping on a bed of nails. This sort of submissiveness to literary discourse is doubly astonishing because, with the exception of children and madmen, it's clear as day to everyone that behind this very discourse lies merely the lifeless reflection of reality — a simulacrum. And that's only in the best case. In the worst case, people simply sit around spinning all kinds of yarns, recklessly playing at life, compelling men and women who never existed to perform acts that were never performed. For all intents and purposes, then, they lead millions of conscientious readers up the garden path by solemnly passing off their fictions as times past, even encroaching upon certain prerogatives set aside for superhumans, because what they do is write "so-and-so thought . . . ," or "a thought crossed so-and-so's mind," but just who does one have to be in order to know precisely what someone thought and precisely what thought crossed someone's mind?

Indeed, sometime you'll open a little tome and read: "In the beginning of July, at an extraordinarily hot time of day, toward evening, a young man walked out of the tiny room he was renting from some tenants of S— Lane into the street, and slowly, as though in a state of indecision, he proceeded in the direction of K— Bridge . . ." That's what you read, and you think: but there never existed the hot July, the evening into which the young man walked from his tiny room, or the tiny room, or S— Lane, or even the young man himself; rather, all of this was thought up by the writer so-and-so to rid himself of his daydreams and earn enough for a buttered roll. Well, fine, let's suppose the hot July did exist, it's possible, and S— Lane and the tiny room rented from the tenants existed as well, but there was never even a trace of any young man. And even if there had been, he never walked out to the street toward evening in the direction of the aforementioned bridge, and even if he had, then it wasn't "as though in a state of indecision" but, on the contrary, in a military step, and not out of his tiny room, and not toward evening, and not in the beginning of July, but out of the barracks of the Izmailovsky Imperial Guards Regiment early on the morning of September 30.

What's more interesting is that for some reason today's standards preclude such insights in our country, and we believe just as unconditionally in literature as our ancestors did in Judgment Day. This cultural phenomenon might be explained by the fact that ours is an evangelical literature, so to speak, although the following should also be considered: that what is depicted is exactly what happened, that in actual fact there had been a hot July, and an evening, and a young man who, precisely "as though in a state of indecision," had set out from a courtyard. It happened if not in the 1860s, then in the 1740s, or under Boris Godunov, or two years ago, because a person lives such a long and richly varied life that there is no situation so desperately literary, or even fantastic, in which a real person hasn't found himself at one time or another. Just as there has yet to be a fantasy that couldn't become reality, just as there is no cause that wouldn't produce its effects, just as there cannot exist a combination of consonants and vowels that couldn't signify something or other in one of the human languages, so, too, there has yet to appear an artistic fabrication that would resonate so little with real situations and affairs that it couldn't possibly be taken for the truth. The whole point, then, is that all of it happened: Yevgeny Onegin and Tatyana Larina, Akaky Akakievich with his ill-fated overcoat, Captain Lebyadkin with his fantastic verse, and Leskov's "Singlethought," except they bore different names, faced different circumstances, lived not exactly then and not exactly there, although these differences are inconsequential. What's important is something else: namely, that in all probability literature is the root of life, so to speak, if not life itself, only slightly displaced along the x-axis, and consequently it should come as no surprise that in Russia where life goes literature follows, but also that where literature goes life follows, that Russians not only write what they live but in part live what they write, that literature has such spiritual authority here, in certain romantic instances it may occur to a completely reasonable person that Alyosha Karamazov wouldn't behave in such a way. And there's positively nothing to be ashamed of when in certain romantic instances we nod and glance back at those figures we hold sacred in the works of Tolstoy, Dostoevsky, or Chekhov, for they are not figments of the imagination, but the true saints of Russian life, having existed in actual fact as exemplars, worthy of imitation in how they suffered and reasoned, for the whole point is that all of it happened. Just what, one wonders, is so inimitably savage about the following scene?: "She cried out, though very weakly, and suddenly her whole weight sank to the floor, yet she still managed to raise both hands to her head . . . Blood gushed as out of an overturned tumbler, and her body fell over backward . . . She was already dead. Her eyes bulged, as if they might pop out, and her forehead and whole face were wrinkled and distorted by a spasm . . . Her skull was smashed to pieces and even displaced a little to the side . . ." This scene has not only occurred in all of the stated details in real life many times over, it's even occurred yet again just recently. True, the circumstances weren't particularly bloody: the sacrificial old lady in a dark piebald coat of an old-fashioned fabric and cut, wearing a funny little fur hat with an ear-band and a pair of felt-and-rubber boots commonly referred to as "farewell youth," was just sitting on a bench at the very top of Pokrovsky Boulevard, having closed her eyes and folded her hands on her stomach — the ways of the last quarter of the twentieth century have succeeded in tempering the classical scene.

It seemed the old woman was snoozing in the sun, which had peeked out for the first time that spring. Two little boys sporting knapsacks sat down next to her on their way home from school and, swinging their legs, chatted a little. Two pigeons nearly touched down by her boots, but then suddenly took flight, flapping their wings in a panic. A passerby in an astrakhan "diplomat" hat asked the old woman how to get to Solianka Street and, getting no reply, said: "Deaf as a doorknob!"

Twilight was already falling, but the old woman kept sitting on the bench without so much as a thought of leaving.

Her appearance on Pokrovsky Boulevard was preceded by a history of sorts, which had unfolded in the great building at the corner of Petroverigsky Lane, in Apartment No. 12, where that famous type of communal apartment dweller was once formed, now little by little disappearing into non-existence. He was formed intricately and not all at once, but rather over almost exactly as much time as Apartment 12 itself had existed. The first to take up residence here was Sergei Vladimirovich Pumpiansky, a Latin teacher at Moscow Gymnasium No. 6. He had a wife, Zinaida Alexandrovna, born Sarantseva, a distant descendant of the same Yelena Ivanovna Sarantseva who was the captain of the only cavalry subunit of its kind, a company of Amazons formed by Potemkin in Balaklava on the occasion of the arrival of Catherine II. Sergei Vladimirovich also had four children: Sergei, Vladimir, Georgy, and Alexandra. Sergey Sergeyevich perished way back in the imperialist war during the summer offensive of 1917; in '34 Vladimir Sergeyevich got himself run over by a local train at the Mamontovka Station, which is on the Yaroslavl line; Georgy Sergeyevich disappeared without a trace in November of '41, during the battle for Moscow, in which he took part as a member of the Home Guard; and Alexandra Sergeyevna held out until our day. Counting from the entrance hall, she occupied the very farthest room in Apartment 12, situated alongside the kitchen and the back door, where the Pumpianskys' cook, Elizaveta, had lived until 1919. This room was small and dark since one of its little windows looked out onto the back staircase, whereas the other — the one over the door — onto the kitchen, which is why in Pumpianskaya's room the light was practically always on. By the period under discussion here, Alexandra Sergeyevna was one of those cultured little old ladies with a thin face who was very well groomed and always gave off an aura of fragrant whiteness.

In the second year of the imperialist war, when the difficulties of daily life had only just begun, the teacher Pumpiansky took ill with dropsy and was forced to take in lodgers. In 1915, the trolley conductor Fondervyakin moved into the room one door down and across the hall from the cook's quarters, the former nursery, along with his wife Agrafena and son Boris, a weak, sickly little fellow. The elder Fondervyakins didn't live for very long, and some time after his parents' demise Boris brought a wife into the apartment, and in '28 they brought into the world their own son, Lev, who remains in good health to date. Lev Borisovich Fondervyakin is a big man with a vast bald patch that looks as if it were lacquered. He's sociable, a bachelor, in that he buried his mother and father but for some reason never settled down to married life himself, and he has a slight lisp that has him pronouncing "since" as "thinth." Lev Borisovich does have one amusing passion: he adores preserving foods — dehydrating, salting, smoking, dry-curing, marinating — and his room gives off the pungent odors of a root cellar.

Soon after the Fondervyakins, Artillery Ensign Ostroumov moved into Apartment 12, occupying the room next door, along the left side of the corridor; he shot himself dead during the February Revolution. In his place, the family of Nikanor Sidorov — a salesclerk at the Alshvang shoe shop on Kuznetsky Bridge and a widower with two unusually large sons — settled in the room. Then the Sidorovs started to die off, marry, breed, and disperse, and in the end the shoe salesman's granddaughter, Vera Alexandrovna Valenchik, was left to reside in the Pumpianskys' former bedroom with her husband, Genrikh Ivanovich Valenchik. Wherever the rest of the Sidorov clan got to has been shrouded by time. Today, Vera Alexandrovna is a forty-year-old woman, a youthful bottle-blonde with a bun in the oven, as they say, whereas Genrikh Ivanovich is a rather short, brawny fellow with a sharply receding hairline and a fastidiously trimmed thin moustache and sideburns. He writes verse and prose in his spare time, knows how to prepare several dishes excellently, and when conversing he repeatedly jabs his interlocutor with his elbow, the way clowns do when they're telling stupid jokes or divulging secrets.

At the very beginning of the 1920s, at the time of the so-called consolidation of the Moscow gentry and bourgeoisie, they crammed as many working folk as they could into Apartment 12, leaving the Pumpiansky family only one room, the former dining room, into which they dragged so much furniture there was barely room enough to shove your way through. The first to move into the former living room, situated on the left of the corridor and adjoining the Sidorovs', was the large family of handyman Popovsky, who spent his time repairing kerosene and Primus stoves. They were followed by the unmarried policeman Konovalov, who perished during the liquidation of the Krasavchik gang, then a quiet worker for the People's Commissariat of Communications and his wife, who suffered from epilepsy, then a political instructor for the Workers' and Peasants' Red Army, Gorizontov, along with his mother and sister, then some incomprehensible fellow who was never home, until finally, right after the monetary reforms of '61, the young engineer Vladimir Leonidovich Golova made this room his home. For a time he led a solitary existence, then he got married, fathered two children, got divorced, and moved away, thus leaving the room to his grass widow Yuliya — a slight woman, dainty, indeed toy-like

— his daughter Lyubov, a girl of thirteen, and his son Pyotr, a serious, sort of intellectual, chubby tyke.

As for the rooms situated along the right side of the corridor . . . as mentioned earlier, at the beginning of the '20s they housed the Pumpiansky family in the former dining room, neighboring Elizaveta the cook's tiny room, where they did indeed live as long as they constituted a family. But with time the Pumpianskys began to disappear, and when Alexandra Sergeyevna was left all alone in the world, they moved her into the cook's tiny room, while its inhabitants, the family of a weaver for the Trëkhgorka Textile Mill, Semyon Timofeyevich Nachalov, were moved into the former dining room, where this weaver then took root and branched out. These days, the room is inhabited exclusively by his daughter-in-law, Anna Olegovna Kapitonova, and her grandson, Mitya Nachalov, a bombastic ninth-grader — sandy-haired, clever-eyed, neat as a pin, and a stickler for detail to the point of pedantry. Mitya's grandfather died in 1954, his mother divorced his father a long time ago, married a Finn and left the country, whereas his father was recruited for the construction of the Kolyma hydroelectric plant.

The former office of the teacher Pumpiansky, just beyond the former dining room, was divided by a partition. Employees of the housing and public services department, such as sanitary technicians, supervisory technicians, electricians — unattached, uncomplicated folk — always lived in the closer half, while in '79 Vasily Chinarikov, the caretaker, took up residence here once and for all. First he worked as the building's caretaker, then he fought in Afghanistan, and then he studied at Moscow University's Department of Philosophy, but only made it to his third year before quitting and going back to being the caretaker. By and large, Vasya Chinarikov is a strong, well-built man, except for a slight limp. He keeps his hair short, dresses in any old thing, and has a rather coarse-looking face — vulgar, as they say, but illuminated from within as if by some playful thought.

In the farther half of the former office for a long time lived Kulakov, an officer of the criminal investigation department, before whom the whole of Apartment 12 trembled, and it's no wonder: he'd somehow managed to detain political instructor Gorizontov in a forced labor facility for a whole week because the instructor had unintentionally caused a short circuit. After Kulakov, two sisters in their declining years moved in. They led such a meek and imperceptible existence that none of the tenants knew them by name. Then around the same time as Chinarikov, Nikita Ivanovich Belotsvetov took the room. A man of about forty-five and a pharmacologist by profession, his outward appearance doesn't easily lend itself to description. It's about as ordinary an appearance as can be, more collective than distinctive, though he does have an unusually large, monumental sort of head. Essentially, Nikita Ivanovich has about as much of a face as you can see in the profile of a head of state on a coin.

What ought to be introduced now are the common areas of Apartment No. 12 and its general topography, as it's indispensable to the story that follows. The front entrance to the apartment has two sets of double-leaf doors: the outer set is painted a shabby brown color and opens outward, the inner ones are upholstered in green leatherette and open inward. There's a dust-covered tiny window above the doors. The entrance hall is fairly spacious: when you go in, there's an antique mirror to the left, grown dull over time and reaching nearly up to the ceiling; to the right, patched up in two places with electrical tape, is the telephone, which is on a bamboo bookcase; a tin can that once contained Spanish asparagus, now intended for cigarette butts, occupies the middle shelf, while the bottom shelf houses a telephone book, as well as a few directories and bills; the wall around the bookcase is covered with telephone numbers, incomprehensible notations, and names of some kind. The doors of two rooms, Belotsvetov's and Chinarikov's, come out onto the entrance hall, beyond which begins the corridor.

The corridor in Apartment 12 is narrow, high-ceilinged, and as dark as a crevice in a glacier. On the left it begins with a door, behind which Yuliya Golova lives with her brood, and farther down there's a neglected wardrobe in which are kept various worthless articles of clothing, whetstones, assorted tools, nails, a few bound sets of the journal *Red Field*, two old electricity meters, and a leaky copper teapot. Farther along the wall hangs Fondervyakin's galvanized washtub, and situated just beyond it is the room occupied by the Valenchiks — the same room in which Artillery Ensign Ostroumov shot himself dead once upon a time. Farther down stands Fondervyakin's fridge, and then comes Fondervyakin's door, at which point the corridor turns ninety degrees to the right, producing the bathroom and toilet, equipped with small windows above their respective doors, and from here it empties into the kitchen. All that is situated along the right side of the corridor are the room occupied by Mitya Nachalov and his grandmother and the sidewall of Alexandra Sergeyevna Pumpianskaya's room, whose other sidewall butts up against the back door.

The kitchen of Apartment 12 is spacious to the point of being festive, even though there are seven kitchen tables lined up against its walls, along with seven shelves and two gas stoves. To the right are a sink, the door to Pumpianskaya's room, and the door onto the back stairwell, which has long since reeked of dampness, fried onions, and kerosene, all combining into a single rank medley.

2

The tenants of Apartment 12 had disliked Alexandra Sergeyevna Pumpianskaya since time immemorial and always oppressed her in whatever way possible. They had no grounds whatsoever for doing this if, of course, you discount her being a nitpicking old woman — full of herself, as the saying goes — and then tidy besides, in that mechanically tidy way so abhorrent to our heart and which we find so hard to bear. Incidentally, it should not be overlooked that Alexandra Sergeyevna could arouse in her neighbors a rudimentary class hostility since, like it or not, she was by birth the proprietress of Apartment 12, of the whole two hundred and forty square meters of living space, and if this was something she never spoke about openly, she nevertheless walked up and down the corridor, switched the lights on and off, took readings off the electricity meter, and swept the kitchen floor in the very same way as would the sole and uncontested proprietress. Alexandra Sergeyevna even fanned the flames of dampened class hostility by continuing to call Kuybyshev by it's pre-revolutionary name of Samara; she was suspected of not acknowledging the new orthography, and once, in reference to Tsar Nicholas the Bloody, said His Majesty. In the twenties, when people were being ruthlessly ousted to the peripheries of life for stunts like that without so much as a second thought, Alexandra Sergeyevna was meek as a lamb — as if she didn't even exist. In the prewar period she discreetly pretended to equality with the tenants of proletarian origins, while in keeping with the most recent times she behaved, logically, as if she were indeed the sole and uncontested proprietress. Otherwise, Alexandra Sergeyevna was by all indications at least a tolerable old lady, even distinguishing herself somewhat favorably from her neighbors, especially in the morning. While the population of Apartment 12 loafed around disheveled, groggy, and pajama-clad, she would appear in an austere housedress of dark broadcloth, albeit shapeless, but with lace cuffs on the sleeves and an embroidered *vologodsky* collar, hair diligently combed and face lightly rouged — altogether clean in that old-womanish way that evokes a complex sort of tenderness. It was the same when she spoke, which was always in a serene tone of voice, the way boring people read aloud. She had a classical vocabulary, ornamented with archaisms like "pretermit," or "no matter," as in: "No matter that Ivan Ivanovich is foolish, he compensates by being able-bodied."

And here's the interesting part: Alexandra Sergeyevna needed only to disappear for the whole apartment to sense right away that something was missing. Now, if the mirror were removed from the entrance hall, or if the door onto the backstairs were boarded up, or if the odor of fermented fruit stopped exuding from Fondervyakin's room, that's just how the apartment would feel: as if something were missing. No one was yet aware that Pumpianskaya had disappeared for all eternity, but the apartment's common areas were already pervaded by a clear sense that something vital was lacking, like electricity, something light in its movements and poignantly pure.

Alexandra Sergeyevna disappeared on one of those days in the middle of March when the Big Dipper hangs right over your head, on a Friday, late in the evening, at about the time when the television stations sign off for the night. That morning she had appeared in the kitchen before anyone else, as usual, carrying in one hand a teakettle with a whistle and in the other a tiny aluminum saucepan with an egg rolling around in it. No sooner had she gotten down to preparing her old-womanish breakfast than Lev Borisovich Fondervyakin came into the kitchen, stood in front of the window, and lost himself in contemplation of the courtyard, tapping nervously on the windowpane with his fingernails. Mitya's grandmother, Anna Olegovna, a robust woman with violet hair, came in next, and right behind her was Pyotr Golova who, breathing noisily through his nose, climbed onto the stool standing by the sink and started swinging his legs. For a time no one spoke, and then Fondervyakin burst out:

"Well alright, I've earned some time off, but how come Dmitry's nowhere to be seen?" he asked Anna Olegovna out of boredom. "Must be time for school."

"I've allowed Mitya to skip his first two classes today," Anna Olegovna announced, tidying her violet ringlets.

"You're spoiling your grandson," Fondervyakin said.

"Spoiling is unavoidable in my position," replied Anna Olegovna. "Without spoiling, our Soviet granny is no longer a granny, but a . . . I don't even know what. Especially since Mitya's been spending entire evenings cobbling something together, so he needs his sleep. Yesterday, for example, he was up till midnight mysteriously busy with some bits of glass."

"One of my workmates," said Fondervyakin, "had a boy who was always mysteriously busy in the evenings too, and it turned out he was a counterfeiter."

"Curse that tongue of yours!" said Anna Olegovna.

"Alright, now," Alexandra Sergeyevna joined in, "one has earned his time off, the other is a truant, but what about this one?" And she pointed a wet finger at Petka, who was still sitting on the stool swinging his legs.

The teakettle whistled nastily, and Alexandra Sergeyevna, the expression on her face having changed from one of anger to anxiety, turned off the stove.

"For the time being he's enjoying a happy childhood," explained Fondervyakin. "Although it's a wonder he doesn't attend some sort of preschool. Pyotr, why don't you attend preschool?"

Pyotr grew morose, silently considered the question, and then started to explain why kindergarten was uninteresting for him, how everything was a routine, according to a schedule, and you had to do what the teacher wanted and not what you wanted.

"For example, we went for a walk in the woods," he lamented, "and the teacher says to us: 'Nothing is allowed. No picking the flowers, no breaking any branches, no trampling the grass . . .' "

"So then what the heck can you do?" an interested Fondervyakin asked him.

"The teacher said, 'You may only admire.' "

Fondervyakin spat symbolically and proclaimed: "They've over-regulated life, the sons of bitches! What a people, trying to impose a resolution every time somebody sneezes. One thing isn't allowed, another's prohibited, this isn't recommended, and that — don't even think about it!"

"Nonetheless," Anna Olegovna interrupted, "I reckon shirking kindergarten won't do."

"It stands to reason," agreed Fondervyakin. "But do you remember,

Citizens, the fellow from Apartment 22 who kept pasting up those outrageous scraps of paper all over the building saying things like, 'No shouting,' 'Don't play with matches,' and 'Handshaking has been abolished'? He died, the scoundrel! Went to visit his sister-in-law in Ulan-Ude and died! Now, by the way, a regular war's flared up in Apartment 22 over his room."

"No wonder," said Anna Olegovna, "the way life is these days they'd slaughter you over two square meters, but then again, doing without those extra meters is like having to do without air sometimes — it's an impossible situation."

"That's for sure," Fondervyakin agreed. "Take me, for example, I've got no place at all to put my sixteen jars of preserved apples, I'm practically sleeping on them. Then there's Vera Valenchik walking around in her seventh month, and Yulka Golova and her kids huddled their in tiny quarters — that's a third case. No, all in all Apartment 22 got lucky: a man has nobly vacated his living space and a fight has broken out over it — an interesting event in and of itself, but somebody may well get a few useful extra meters, which anybody would be glad to get their hands on."

Here Fondervyakin paused deliberately, then gave Alexandra Sergeyevna a comical look and continued:

"And meanwhile some citizens, whose time for eternal rest is long overdue, persist in occupying useful meters and think it's the most natural thing in the world!"

Alexandra Sergeyevna didn't take Fondervyakin's words personally, since at that moment she was worried about overcooking her egg.

"Those useful meters," said Anna Olegovna, "would come in handy for me and Mitya, too. Here I am with a lad who's already fully grown, yet he has to go on and on sharing a room with an old woman."

"For pity's sake, Anna Olegovna, you're hardly an old woman!" objected Fondervyakin. "You are a woman in the prime of life! Now, some citizens — yes ma'am, some citizens have positively lived too long. How are you feeling, there, Alexandra Sergeyevna, you unbelievable person?"

Pumpianskaya took this question at face value and candidly answered:

"Poorly, Lev Borisovich, good for nothing, really. I ache all over, I've only to think of something and it hurts. And you wouldn't believe the silly things I imagine sometimes."

"Then you should undergo treatment," suggested Anna Olegovna blackly, and fixed her violet ringlets for the second time.

Whereupon Mitya Nachalov entered the kitchen, not quite awake, with a bath towel over his shoulder.

"It's too late for me to undergo treatment," responded Alexandra Sergeyevna, and she picked up her dishes. "I've expended my vital forces. Whenever I begin to feel unwell, I go out into the fresh air straight away — and that's the extent of my treatment. And I am beyond taking pills. I fear my demise is only one bad cold away."

At that moment, Mitya's face assumed a thoughtful expression, as though he'd only just then awoken. Alexandra Sergeyevna, having had her say, went to her room with her teakettle and tiny saucepan jiggling slightly in her hands. Anna Olegovna left right behind her, the smell of pearl barley accompanying her out.

"Listen, Dima," said Fondervyakin, "our old lady's in a very bad way, already imagining things . . ."

"So what?" asked Mitya.

"So, it's about time we thought about redistributing living space because it looks as if she'll be departing this life any minute."

"Her? That'll be the day," observed Mitya. "Chances are she'll outlive us both. You know what these pre-revolutionary old-timers are like — cast-iron constitutions!"

"No, Dmitry, the time has come to give it some thought, or else a grueling war will break out later, like what's happened in Apartment 22. Why should you care, you're unattached as can be, but the Valenchiks are expecting a new arrival. And again, I've got no place to put my sixteen jars of preserved apples . . ."

"So then the room will go to you."

"What makes you think that?" Fondervyakin joyously asked Mitya.

"Because Valenchik's the sucker around here!"

"I don't understand your idiotic language . . ."

"Come on, he's a dupe! How can he not be a dupe when his wife two-times him even while she's pregnant?!"

"Oh, don't gossip!

"What gossip, I've seen it with my own eyes! And I'm not the only one — Pumpianskaya's spotted her with Vaska Chinarikov. I'll keep my mouth shut, but Pumpianskaya will snitch."

"Ech, they should stick the old woman in a nursing home!"

"The three of you should do it, you and . . . Send her packing."

"Why the three of us?"

"You, because of your sixteen jars of preserved apples, Valenchik, the sucker, because he's expecting a new arrival, and Vaska Chinarikov, because Pumpianskaya will snitch on him."

"That's logical," said Fondervyakin, and he grew thoughtful.

Mitya went to the bathroom, deftly clicking his extended tongue in conclusion, while Fondervyakin again began to tap the window-pane with his fingernails. After a pause, he said:

"Petka, give us a song . . ."

Pyotr didn't wait for opportunity to knock twice, as the saying goes, and immediately launched into a song that began with the words "The detachment walked along the shore, it had walked from afar," singing it with great solemnity at that.

"Who taught you that?" Fondervyakin asked him when he'd finished.

"Life," said Pyotr.

3

After Mitya Nachalov had left for school, Pumpianskaya and Anna Olegovna had washed the dishes in the kitchen without speaking, Fondervyakin had telephoned some acquaintance, and Pyotr Golova had strolled aimlessly up and down the corridor a few times, a perfect silence enveloped Apartment 12. The tenants had dispersed to their own rooms, and here's who got down to what: Pyotr took a seat by the window and stared vacantly into the alley; Fondervyakin analyzed the Evergreen Game, yawning into his fist from time to time; Anna Olegovna read *Tales from the Don*; Alexandra Sergeyevna used a velvet ribbon to polish her Kuznetsovsk tea service, which Sergei Vladimirovich Pumpiansky himself had acquired way back when from the Muir and Merrilees department store.

Around two o'clock in the afternoon Lyuba Golova came home from school, and Mitya showed up practically right behind her.

Lyuba changed into a lively little smock, fed Pyotr, got him ready for a stroll, kicked him out the door, and then ensconced herself in the kitchen with her Latin textbook.

"What the hell do you need that for?" Mitya asked, pointing at the book.

"Because I do!" Lyuba replied.

"In that case, you should keep your lofty interests to yourself and study in your own room."

Dmitry hovered around Lyuba for a bit, and after a minute he asked:

"Do you think Pumpianskaya understands Latin?"

"I have no idea. Nikita Ivanovich understands it — that much I know for sure."

"We're not talking about Belotsvetov right now. Tell you what, Lyubov, do me a favor . . ." And Mitya's face took on an expression that was at once subtly pensive and cruel, an expression so meaningful that Lyuba's little eyes began to gleam, and out of impatience she even parted her lips ever so slightly. But Mitya didn't have a chance to finish what he was saying. It was dinnertime, and at almost the very same moment he was about to make his request the kitchen filled up with the principal characters who'd recently appeared, plus Vasily Chinarikov, who in the meanwhile had returned from his caretaker's post in the yard some time after two, and minus Pumpianskaya, who took a late dinner, *à l'européenne*. So Mitya and Lyubov went into the corridor to finish their conversation.

"Listen, Vasily," said Fondervyakin, addressing Chinarikov, and trying not to lapse into sarcasm, "our Pumpianskaya's in complete decline, she'll be kicking the bucket any day now. Her little room wouldn't come in handy to you by any chance, would it?"

"Strictly speaking," answered Chinarikov, "that would be a pantry, not a room."

"Even if it is just a pantry," Anna Olegovna stepped in, "hand it over to me anyway!"

"Do as you please," said Fondervyakin, "but I, Fellow Citizens, am giving you honorable notice that I'm in the process of gathering all the necessary documents to get the little room transferred over to me."

"Where do you get the idea that Pumpianskaya's going to kick the bucket any day now?" Chinarikov asked distractedly, and with those words he left the kitchen.

"Instead of talking all kinds of nonsense, Lev Borisovich," said Anna Olegovna, "you'd better work on your pronunciation — it's sickening to listen to sometimes, as if you were mimicking somebody."

This remark cut Fondervyakin to the quick. He hung around the kitchen a bit longer so as not to betray his resentment and then he went back to his room, slamming the door shut behind him.

Anna Olegovna decided to tell Pyotr off at the same time:

"Since when have you been in the habit of sitting around the kitchen day in day out listening to adult conversations?!"

Pyotr crawled down off the stool and began sidling backward, in the direction of the corridor.

"No, you wait a minute! Answer me: are you stuck here like a fly on honey, or what? And another thing: why did you sprinkle magnesium carbonate in Alexandra Sergeyevna's tea yesterday . . . ?"

But Pyotr was long gone, the spot where he'd just been standing now an empty space.

After dinner, Apartment 12 quieted down again. At five o'clock

Pumpianskaya went to the kitchen and began preparing her dinner, which consisted of a diced beet and potato salad dressed with mayonnaise, onion soup, and a small lamb cutlet, steamed. As the old woman dawdled over her dinner, Mitya Nachalov called her to the phone. She hurried to take the receiver, but whoever was on the other end had decided not to speak.

Some time after six that evening Nikita Ivanovich Belotsvetov came home from work and started to drag himself around the kitchen with such tense melancholy on his face it was as though he were lying in wait for someone. Pumpianskaya came out of her room to fill up a small porcelain gravy boat with water, and Belotsvetov nodded to her. Fondervyakin peeped meditatively into the kitchen, twice, looking for someone to talk to, but Belotsvetov was silent, keeping an eye on his gas stove. Anna Olegovna Kapitonova proceeded toward the backstairs, Belotsvetov still keeping his silence. Finally, Yuliya Golova appeared in an over-sized terrycloth bathrobe, looking like a cocooned silkworm, and Belotsvetov gave a start.

"Listen, Yuliya!" he said. "I wish you'd keep a tighter rein on your Petka. He smeared my door handle with some kind of muck today, little devil . . . ! I think it was mustard, or something like that."

Yuliya smiled guiltily, not knowing how to respond, and just then Vasily Chinarikov sauntered into the kitchen in a pair of well-worn jeans and a sleeveless undershirt, revealing an airborne forces tattoo on his left shoulder, and his entrance saved Yuliya from having to make a saccharine apology.

"What are we kicking up a fuss about?" Chinarikov asked and lit a crude *papirosa*.

"Well, you see, Petka Golova smeared my door handle with some kind of muck! I think it was mustard, or something like that . . ."

"Forget it, Nikita," said Chinarikov. "It's ludicrous to flare up over such trifles."

"Why, I'm not . . . that is . . . flaring up because Petka smeared my door handle, but because he's such an expert at playing dirty tricks."

Yuliya seized the opportunity to steal away.

"You see, here's the situation," continued Belotsvetov, "I mean, it's terrible when a person is capable of conscious villainy even in early childhood."

"Come to your senses, Nikita," said Chinarikov, a look of cheerful commiseration on his face. "What do you mean by 'conscious villainy'?! Foolishness, mischief, bad manners — that, yes . . ."

"Well, the fact is, even the most savage crimes stem from foolishness, mischief, and bad manners — in a word, these very trifles! You know, it's not so much the savage crimes that depress me, as . . . I mean, they depress me, of course, but not like one's capacity for conscious villainy even in early childhood. Here's where I sense the secret and the solution to all mysteries, here lies fertile ground for the very seeds of evil."

"Why the hell do you even care about these seeds?!"

"I'll explain straightaway. You see, Vasily, I'm at the end of my rope! I've spent forty-five years of my life living peaceably side-by-side with villainy, but no more, something inside me has flipped over! I just can't handle looking at liver-spotted kissers anymore, or listening to hyper-intellectual conversations on various earth-shattering issues such as 'whatever happened to elastic waistbands,' or watching the beaten, robbed, and deceived anymore — I don't intend to tolerate life's insults any longer, period. And do you know how it all started . . . ?"

Chinarikov grew attentive.

"The day before yesterday I'm walking past our grocery store and I see an elderly woman standing by the wall. I look at her, and you know, it was as if I'd been kicked in the gut. Her clothes looked like she'd picked them out of a garbage can. She had two mismatched men's boots on — imagine that: two mismatched men's boots, one black, the other brown! . . . and some unbelievable hat — to make a long story short, it was an unprecedented, almost fantastical scene for a Soviet city at the end of the 1980s! But this is still nothing by comparison. The most frightening thing about her was that she'd been beaten up on top of it all: her lower lip was scabbed over, she had a huge shiner under one eye and was covering the other one with a handkerchief, and that handkerchief — get this, old friend — is snow-white. Although what frightened me most were not the marks left by the beating, but that she wasn't some utter down-and-out, or a madwoman, or some alky, she was an ordinary elderly woman, only ridiculously dressed. Her handkerchief told me that. And the most important thing, of course, is that no one was paying any attention to her, as if it were perfectly natural for a beaten-up woman to be standing in front of a grocery store in broad daylight not three kilometers from Red Square, wearing two mismatched men's boots.

"And there you go. I looked at her and my heart sank. So there I am, standing opposite her, blocking pedestrian traffic, at which point she turns around to face me: 'Pumpkin-head,' she says . . . no, get a load of this — barely alive herself, yet she's calling me names . . ."

"By the way, she was right on the mark," said Chinarikov, smiling. "A very fitting nickname."

" 'Pumpkin-head,' she says, 'lead me home, 'cause my legs are too weak to walk.' Naturally, I took her by the arm and started to lead her. But lead her where? This I couldn't figure out because first she's talking about Armenian Lane, then about the Novogireevo metro station, then about the reunification of the Ukraine with Russia. And lo and behold, that's when the most important thing happened: I came to hate the old bat . . . Why is this the most important thing? Because in my view, it was precisely this hatred that brought about the profound upheaval inside me. You've got to carefully consider my position at the time: first, I pitied her to such an extent that the only reason I didn't cry was because crying on the street is unacceptable, it would be taken the wrong way; second, a sense of wounded nationalism was awakened within me, as the old bat's outward appearance is a sheer insult to the nation; third, I was obliged to take her away to wherever it was she needed to go; fourth, I hated her — hated her for the fact of hating her, hated her because walking alongside her was horribly awkward, because taking her to wherever it was she needed to go was practically impossible, and because I'd gotten pretty sick of her. I'm walking along and saying to myself: 'As it turns out, old boy, you are a heel! Or even better, since you're a heel, then act like it, break the hell away from this old bat and duck into the first gateway that comes along!' And that's just what I did, although you know, Vasya, I'm really not a heel at all.

"It's already been three days and I can't forget about her; her image haunts me, like a ghost . . . ! All in all it feels like I've fallen good and sick, mentally. The main thing is that for three days running I've felt a sort of stifling tear ripening in my soul . . ."

"The way I see it, you really have fallen sick, Nikita."

"Maybe I have, except this sickness is dearer to me now than any kind of practical health. I've now reached the boiling point and I intend to fight tooth and nail against evil of any kind!"

"That's absurd!" said Chinarikov, lighting another *papirosa*. "You're just like a little child, Nikita, my God! Good and evil exist, I would even say coexist, in the same way as fire and water, heaven and earth, man and woman . . . If there were no evil, there would be no struggle or movement, which is to say — life."

"That's all just philosophy," said Belotsvetov.

"No, Nikita, it's not philosophy yet, but your ABC's. Here's what philosophy is . . . According to John Damascene, evil is non-existence — in other words, the simple absence of good; according to Mandeville, it's an indispensable tool for the construction of the world; according to Socrates, it's happenstance, the existence of which can be explained by the fact that people haven't got a clue about what's good or what's bad; according to Thomas Aquinas, everything is good, and evil just its shabby component. Leibniz generally maintains that evil is simply underdeveloped good, that a measure of necessary evil is in humans' not being able to fly and birds being denied the gift of speech. Finally, I personally consider that evil, as such, doesn't exist, that what exists instead is an attitude toward evil. If, for example, I'm tormented by a lack of money, fools, and ragged old bats, then they're evil, but if my attitude toward them is one of indifference, then they're neither good nor evil, but a void. In sum, getting irate at evil is absurd, but wrestling with it — that's a sickness. Evil is elemental, like a tsunami or an earthquake, so everyday reasoning tells you that all you need is to work out the appropriate attitude toward it, as with a tsunami or an earthquake, or with anything elemental."

"I can't agree with that, and here's the reason why: evil is very simple — so simple, Vasya, it's a wonder nearly everyone doesn't commit it! The reality is that not even close to everyone commits it, certainly not the majority, and not even the minority, but rather an *insignificant* minority. This means evil doesn't coexist on equal terms with its opposites — good and the void — in other words, it's unnatural, illicit!"

"Well, not even close to everyone's head works that way, certainly not the majority's! The majority uses its intuition, while maybe two people on each hemisphere actually use their heads."

"Okay, let's assume that's no argument."

"Fine, here's an argument for you," Chinarikov said, energetically motioning with his head. "Irrespective of whatever percentage of people murder, steal, commit acts of violence and so on, evil continues to exist — it always has and always will, which means it's part and parcel of human nature, which means it's natural. If in one and a half million years people have been unable to do anything about evil, regardless of their seeming preoccupation with this one issue alone, then that means it's natural . . . !"

"What are you on about, boys?" asked Fondervyakin insinuatingly. He'd come into the kitchen somehow without being noticed.

"Vasily and I are keeping this between ourselves, Lev Borisovich, please excuse us . . ."

Fondervyakin looked at both of them suspiciously, wriggled his lips a little, and left.

Chinarikov continued:

"You see, Nikita, people have devised remedies for everything

— pestilence, hydrophobia, overproduction crises, droughts, locusts — and now as before, the only thing there's no remedy for is evil."

"What do you mean? There is so . . . Renounce your sense of self, your ego, and you'll be as harmless as a kitten. Because the only thing fraught with evil is what emanates from the ego, from personal interests, which don't always or necessarily make common cause with the laws of goodness. But for some reason this renunciation is impossible, even though it promises almost complete personal security, and immortality as well."

"That's the whole point, such remedies are suited only to a handful — chiefly to those who devise them. By and large, Christ propounded a fairly uncomplicated path for the healing of humankind, and Tolstoy, it would seem, devised a means of wrestling with evil within everyone's grasp, through the renunciation of any struggle whatsoever against evil — that is, appeasement — the problem being, of course, that they measured human life by their own standards, even though each was one of a kind! Meanwhile, what's needed is a remedy like aspirin, something that would serve millions."

"Have I got a provocative idea as far as that goes! You see, I suspect that the bulk of villainies that cannot be traced either to human weakness, upbringing, or circumstances of the social order, stems from some dark psychosis, some as yet unclassified variety of schizophrenia. In other words, such villains are simply insane. And that's why I propose combating them with medication. Here, you decide: can a person really be called mentally fit if he beats up an old bat because he was in a bad mood, or sends ten thousand soldiers to their death only because he did poorly in school, or sends his political opponent to the scaffold for preferring the Old Indian opening to the Queen's Gambit — is such a person not mentally ill?! And the specialists ask him: 'What's today's date?' 'How many fingers have you got all together?' — and if he answers what today's date is and how many fingers he's got, then the specialists have no concerns whatsoever about his mental health. In a word, the solution to all problems might lie in working out a suitable medication containing catecholamines, which you then pack into ampoules or tablets, like acetylsalicylic acid, for example."

"Now that's sounds like some kind of utopian idealism, old boy, absolutely repulsive just to listen to!"

"It's not any kind of idealism at all!" said Belotsvetov testily. "For your information, I've already done a little reckoning."

"To make a long story short, Professor, there's a host of teachings out there about how to make a person out of a person, yet Petka Golova smeared your door handle with some kind of muck today . . . Well, if it isn't him in the flesh — speak of the devil!"

Pyotr walked into the kitchen carrying an empty frying pan, and after meeting Belotsvetov's edifying gaze, he recoiled toward Fondervyakin's table.

"Pyotr," Belotsvetov appealed to him, "why are you making a nuisance of yourself? Why did you mess up my door handle?!"

Pyotr said nothing.

"Are you being spoken to or not?" said Chinarikov, backing Belotsvetov up with a hilarious expression on his face instead of the ferocious, albeit paternal, one he had intended.

"Did you see me messing it up?" asked Pyotr unhurriedly. "Have you got any witnesses?"

"What a stinker!" said Chinarikov in outrage. "Has yet to learn a single letter of the alphabet but already knows all the basic legal ploys!"

At these words Alexandra Sergeyevna Pumpianskaya joined the company and, owing to her advanced age, made the announcement of no interest to anyone that no more than forty minutes ago she had been called to the phone, but it seemed no one was on the line. Genrikh Valenchik turned up in the kitchen after her, and then Fondervyakin, so Belotsvetov led Chinarikov to his room to finish their conversation, Chinarikov continuing the argument in route without waiting for the more favorable setting.

"What is all the philosophy in the world really worth," he said, "if it's unable to answer the simplest of questions: why it is that in some Stuttgart or other you can't get belted in the mouth just for the hell of it, while over here it's a free for all . . . !"

Shortly after Chinarikov's voice had died out at the far end of the corridor, and immediately after Pumpianskaya had left for her own room, Genrikh Valenchik assumed an air of confidentiality, that is, he puffed himself up somewhat conspiratorially and said:

"I've got accurate information that says any time now our old lady will be kicking the bucket. I propose we hold a meeting on the subject of who the freed-up living space will be going to."

"It'll be going to me," said Fondervyakin, "I'm notifying you of that right now, without any meetings."

"Well then, we'll just go ahead and examine your pretensions to the dwelling right now, collectively! Or do you oppose yourself to public opinion? Bear in mind, we will not tolerate such unbridled individualism — you can be sure of that!"

Valenchik looked at Fondervyakin sternly and went off to assemble the residents. Five minutes later the entire population of Apartment 12 had packed themselves into the kitchen, with the exception of Pumpianskaya, Chinarikov, and Belotsvetov, to whom the matter was of no importance.

"This is our way, the Soviet way!" said Anna Olegovna Kapitonova with a gleam in her eye. "Happiness, grief, and problems — everything is decided hand in hand! Just like it was during the Olympics . . ."

Everybody recalled how, indeed, during the Moscow Olympics in 1980 Apartment 12 pulled together to put the kibosh on a major scandal that had erupted after Fondervyakin's washtub had tumbled down onto Yuliya Golova's head.

"Come on, Comrades, let's do without the lyricism," asked Valenchik. "Let's stick to the point. A room in the apartment may be freeing up tomorrow, and we've had no communiqué as yet . . ."

"Here's what the communiqué should say," Yuliya Golova joined in. "We're required to come to an agreement right now as to which of us has the indisputable right to an augmentation of their living space."

"We've got more right than anybody," decided Lyuba immediately. "Because there are three of us living together, and what's more we've got a single mother."

"The more so because I'm heterosexual," added Pyotr.

"Seems you're a bit too literate," Fondervyakin said to him.

"No, Comrades, this approach is wrong, too quantitative somehow," said Anna Olegovna, and she proudly shook her violet ringlets. "Let's look at the qualitative side of the affair. My Dmitry is already a young man and he has to go on and on sharing a room with an old woman . . ."

At this point Anna Olegovna looked angrily at Fondervyakin and peremptorily said:

"And don't you even mention your preserved apples, Lev Borisovich!"

"Of course, we ought to let our conscience decide," said Vera Valenchik. "Preserved apples — that's funny, but I'm giving birth soon and that, Comrades, is *not* funny."

"Right!" Mitya spoke up. "Only let's dispense with the demagoguery now that conscience has been dragged into it . . . !"

How the negotiations progressed can be painlessly omitted, since nothing else fundamentally new or meaningful was said, and in general the meeting yielded no decision at all. The only outcome, which emerged independently of the will of the participants, was that it became clear to each of them that even if Alexandra Sergeyevna Pumpianskaya was perfectly healthy, she was obliged to die by morning.

It was some time after ten that evening when the residents dispersed to their own rooms, and the apartment settled down. The drone of television sets could still be heard for a while, and then even that ended. The time had come for things to transpire.

4

Apartment 12 was not yet asleep, only just preparing to turn in. Yuliya Golova was sitting at her dressing table, getting herself ready for bed; Lyubov was making up the beds while, slowly and abhorrently, Pyotr undressed. At the Valenchiks', Vera, having placed a newspaper over her face, was already lying in bed, while Genrikh Ivanovich, bent low over the dining table, set pen to paper and scribbled away. Fondervyakin sat in front of the turned-off television, cutting lid liners for his jars out of a rubber bathmat. Chinarikov was reading the selected speeches of Cicero in his room, and Belotsvetov *The Pharmacology Bulletin* in his. Anna Olegovna was rustling something unpleasantly behind the antique Chinese screen with which she partitioned herself off from Mitya at night, while Mitya messed around at his table, mysteriously busy again with some bits of glass, components, and multicolored wiring. As for Alexandra Sergeyevna Pumpianskaya, she was just sitting on a chair in the middle of her room, out of boredom recalling one evening long ago. It was either 1912 or 1913 — before the war — she was still young, her father, mother, and brothers were still alive; the whole family had gathered in the dining room for tea, it was late in the evening, the dining room was flooded with an even green light, because an electric bulb had been set into the chandelier of aquamarine glass; the grandfather clock, presented to her father for some jubilee celebration in honor of his pedagogical work, ticked grandly; now and then silver teaspoons clinked in Kuznetsovsk teacups; beyond the window the wind howled; Sergei and Vladimir were playing mahjong, while Georgy read Teffi out loud, holding in his left hand a candlestick in the shape of a scooped-out eggshell with a semi-transparent stearin stub in it and choking with laughter after every ten words . . . Good Lord, how marvelous and lovely a recollection!

At about half past ten, Fondervyakin telephoned someone. A little later Mitya Nachalov made a bit of noise in the corridor, then Belotsvetov shuffled through in the direction of the toilet, but no sooner had he turned right than he was struck dumb as the following scene unfolded before his eyes: in the middle of the dark kitchen, in the pale parallelogram formed by the light from the street and the window, sat Pyotr Golova on a chamber pot, holding an unfolded newspaper in front of him. Actually, there wasn't anything so very astonishing about this scene — most likely, Pyotr was simply imitating the male practice of performing these two activities at the same time, but for some reason Belotsvetov was flabbergasted nonetheless.

"Petka, are you all right?" he asked in an unsteady voice.

"Not too bad," said Pyotr, gazing calmly at Belotsvetov from behind the newspaper, and then becoming absorbed, as it were, again in his reading.

In a word, Apartment 12 was not yet asleep, but it was time for things to transpire. God knows whither and whence a little draft flitted across the floor. A few square centimeters of wallpaper, which had come loose in the spot where the neglected wardrobe stood, started to breathe, and over by the bookcase something whispered of its own accord. After that the water pipes joined in, at first ventriloquizing in muted tones then suddenly hushing up, as if someone had cut them short. Bits of lime sprinkled down somewhere, something squeaked — something completely unrecognizable, secret. A floorboard creaked on its own in the kitchen. At this point Genrikh Valenchik came out of his room, and things lay low for a time. Valenchik stuck a cigarette in his mouth, walked up and down the corridor a few times, stood over by Fondervyakin's washtub for a bit, and then returned to his room, shutting the door with a deafening slam. Again the corridor was empty, and again it was time for things to transpire, though not yet at their full potential, as though things were wise to the fact that Pumpianskaya had not yet checked, as was her custom, if the lights had all been switched off.

At a quarter to eleven, a dreadful woman's scream filled the corridor, a wild scream, bestial somehow, the kind the vocal chords might be capable of producing only in those rare instances when a person confronts something too horrible, something on the very peripheries of the perceivable. The apartment was revived at once. The sound of movements and voices came from behind doors, and in the next moment the tenants spilled out of their rooms wearing whatever they'd been able to grab. Halfway down the corridor, in a housecoat with only one button done up, a crookedly hanging chintz nightshirt visible beneath it, stood Yuliya Golova in curlers and gilded Indian slippers, riveted to the spot, her face gray, eyes bulging wide, mouth trembling.

"What the hell are you bawling about?!" asked Fondervyakin spitefully.

Yuliya only half-lifted her arm in the direction of the front door.

"What the heck happened?!" implored Genrikh Valenchik. "Can you tell us in plain language?"

"There . . ." began Yuliya, lifting her hand decisively in the direction of the front door. "A ghost, a man, he was standing there, just now . . ."

Despite the fact that everybody's heart skipped a beat, as the saying goes, when they heard these words, not one of the tenants believed Yuliya. Needless to say, it would have been surprising if anyone had believed her, and yet it was incomparably more surprising still that no one *at all* believed her, for ghosts are the secret passion of our literature, which embeds them in the most poignant situations, and we're nothing if not a literary people who do not even trust in life to the extent we do in novels and stories. Ultimately, Yuliya Golova's situation constituted nothing more than an everyday variation of the situation one allegedly fictional character found himself in one hundred and twenty years ago:

" '. . . By the way, do you believe in ghosts?'

'What kind of ghosts?'

'Commonplace ghosts, what kind do you think!'

'Do you believe in them?'

'Yes and no, I suppose, *pour vous plaire* . . . that is, it's not that I don't . . .'

'Do they appear to you, then?'

'. . . Marfa Petrovna has deigned to visit,' he said, twisting his lips into a strange smile.

'How do you mean, "has deigned to visit"?'

'She's come three times already . . .'

'Were you awake?'

'Very much awake. I was awake all three times. She comes, talks for a minute, then goes out the door, always out the door. I can almost hear it.'

'. . . What does she say to you when she comes?'

'Her? Imagine, such insignificant nonsense it makes you wonder about people, it really makes me mad . . .' "

"You imagined it," said Anna Olegovna soothingly. She'd come out still looking quite decent — in other words, hair kempt and clad in a dressing gown. "You only imagined it, Yuliya. Don't drink strong tea before bed, drink an infusion of valerian root, or take Tazepam — it just magics away those otherworldly . . ."

"Well now, what a fine load of advice that is," observed Belotsvetov, who was dressed anything but casually in slacks, a shirt and tie.

"We've lived to see the day!" said Vera Valenchik. "Now we've got ghosts in the apartment! Not enough cockroaches, so let's have ghosts now! No — when, oh when will they finally tear this multistory fleabag the hell down and accommodate people in comfortable housing with some modern conveniences?"

"I suggest we refer this question to President Reagan," said Genrikh, who was in a fishnet T-shirt and black sateen shorts. "And you, Penelope," this was now addressed to Vera, "off to bed with you, chop-chop. Take a look at what an erotic sight you are — this isn't a cabaret . . . !"

Indeed, Vera Valenchik had jumped out barefoot wearing only a nightgown.

"I don't get it," said Mitya Nachalov, screwing up his eyes scornfully. "How do the Americans figure in this?"

"Because," replied Genrikh, "thanks to the Washingtonian administration we're forced to give up the shirt off our backs for an arms race instead of building comfortable housing!"

"A battle between two worlds," confirmed Fondervyakin with a meaningful look; he was standing not far from his washtub, wrapped in a striped sheet. "By hook or by crook American imperialism is itching to get us. But I'll say this, if for the sake of peace on the planet we'll have to coexist with ghosts — I've got nothing against it."

A taunting look on his face, Chinarikov asked him:

"What do you think, Lev Borisovich, are there not in the Soviet Department of the CIA those responsible for potatoes? I mean, those special agents of imperialism who are responsible for ensuring constant disruptions in the supply of potatoes in our stores?"

"Yes, there are!" answered Fondervyakin, knitting his brows, and he made for his room.

"So, in any case, what's the consensus on this incident with the ghost?" asked Genrikh Valenchik, not addressing any person in particular, and he pulled his hands up into his armpits expressively.

"What sort of consensus can there be . . . ," said Belotsvetov. "It's not like we can call in the Center for Pest and Ghost Control. Still, as your Vera correctly observed, we're not dealing with cockroaches."

"Here's your consensus," added Anna Olegovna. "Strong tea shouldn't be drunk before bed!"

The voice of Pumpianskaya sounded right after these words. She had appeared at the far end of the corridor in her eternal housedress of broadcloth and lace.

"For goodness sake," she said, "the clock says almost midnight, and you're having a full-fledged demonstration here! Has anything happened?"

"There has," answered Mitya. "A ghost appeared. It's an outright Scottish castle, not an apartment . . ."

And everyone began to disperse.

Nothing else interesting happened that evening. Pumpianskaya began her rounds around midnight, checking that all the lights were out and that the door in the entrance hall was locked up good and tight.

By the next morning, she had disappeared.

SATURDAY

1

Though it may seem speculative at first, if not futile, investigating the relationship between life and what we call literature would be useful at this point. The relationship in question is extremely abstruse, so this won't be an easy undertaking, but it is tempting to try nonetheless. First, it's tempting to ascertain to what degree literature is a game and to what a book of fates, a textbook of life. Second, having established these explanatory degrees, it should be possible, at least theoretically, to discover the answers to one or two mysteries of the spirit and of existence, because you never know, it may very well be that literature is uniquely positioned to reveal much more about life than life is about itself. Third, it is well known that literature is existence transformed, refracted through artistic talent, and refracted so truly that you believe more firmly in Pushkin's Tatyana Larina than you do in your next-door neighbor. Finally, if a person were not to live at all — that is, if he were to live, but as an utter hermit, an ascetic who only read lofty books — then here's what is curious: at least it would make for an intriguing life.

Teasing out the relations formed between reality and its artistic hypostasis is helped along by the simplest of equations: $\sqrt{\text{life}} \times \text{talent} = \text{literature}$. It seems we know what life is — the lasting celebration of personal existence; we can imagine what the root of life is — the fruitful celebration of personal existence; it seems we also know what literature is — the same celebration, only shifted along the axes of time and space, the very same celebration, only multiplied by talent. The only value we don't know is what constitutes talent. This, of course, is the x of all x's, such a humble x that there's nothing more comprehensible to say about it other than that talent is every bit a hidden value. Therefore, the mathematical approach will not do in this instance, since in the equation $\sqrt{\text{life}} \times$ talent = literature, the unknown is so profoundly unknown it leaves a gaping, enigmatic space.

That any attempt, no matter how feeble, no matter how documentary, to reconstruct reality by using the tools of literary discourse inevitably turns reality into its opposite, that is, into literature, should give pause for thought. This being the case, the relationships we are looking for must be strictly obligate, perhaps even fated.

Here is another interesting observation: compared to literature, life is much more mottled, incoherent, variable, detailed, tedious. What follows is a bizarre suggestion: perhaps literature is indeed life, in other words, the ideal of its construction, the standard for all weights and measures, while so-called life comprises a sketch, avenues of approach, a blank, and in the most felicitous situations — a version. More than anything it looks as if literature, word of honor, is the fair copy and life a rough copy, and not even the most useful.

It's true that every so often the life of a person sprouts into literature by virtue of some of its particulars, as was the case with Nikolai Uspensky, for example, when in a state of intoxication he would roam from tavern to tavern carrying around a quaint menagerie: his two-year-old daughter and a stuffed crocodile. But this type of occurrence is extremely rare. As a rule, the principle of life is one thing and the principle of literature quite another.

You see how events transpire in literature:

" 'My dear sir,' he began almost solemnly, 'poverty is not a vice, that's the truth. I also know that drunkenness is not a virtue, and this is all the more true. But beggary, dear sir, beggary is a vice, sir. In poverty you still preserve your innate nobility of soul whereas in beggary — nobody, never. For beggary they'll not even chase you out with a stick, but with a broom, swept out of the company of humans so that it's all the more insulting; and rightly so, because in beggary I am ready to be the first to insult myself. Hence, the taverns . . . !' "

Here is how things happen in life . . .

Around seven o'clock on Saturday morning Mitya Nachalov came into the kitchen, which was still deserted, having become somewhat unaccustomed to people overnight, and he began to prepare his breakfast, a rare occurrence, even an exceptional one — an event, even, rather than an occurrence. Soon after, Vasily Chinarikov appeared, carrying past his bare torso, with feeling, on his way to the bathroom. Then Belotsvetov came into the kitchen with a waffled towel wrapped around his throat like a scarf. Then Fondervyakin joined those in the kitchen, astonishing them all, since despite the early hour he was drunk.

"Lev Borisovich, where did you get so pickled?"

"I got pickled right here in the kitchen," answered Fondervyakin, and he sat down heavily on the stool. "I was feeling so miserable I opened a three-liter jar of my preserved apples and here, if you please, is your result. As it turns out, though, drinking in the morning really hits the spot. It's refreshing and altogether . . ."

"Most likely, Lev Borisovich, instead of preserved apples you ended up with plain old moonshine," conjectured Mitya.

"Pickled apples, that's for sure."

"Have you no fear of being so reckless?" smirked Belotsvetov. "Why, moonshine will get you almost as much time in the clink today as high treason!"

"I've had my share of fear, boys," Fondervyakin announced, and he slapped his knees with conviction.

"What a pig-headed public!" Chinarikov joined in as he entered the kitchen. His torso glistened as though it had been oiled, and a necklace of droplets flowed across his chest. "Even on the scaffold it won't renounce its wine-and-vodka-loving convictions! Here, I've got a joke for you. So they tell a moonshiner: 'You'd better close up shop, or they'll run you in.' He goes: 'If they run me in, my son'll cook it up.' They go: 'And your son'll get run in.' Him: 'If my son gets run in, my grandson'll cook it up.' 'Your grandson'll get run in, too.' 'By the time my grandson gets run in,' he goes, 'I'll be getting out.' "

"You keep quiet, you parachutist!" said Fondervyakin, but more comically than with malice.

"I'm not a parachutist," pouted Vasily nevertheless, "but a former Russian soldier of the Soviet Army, and if need be I can prove it beyond any doubt!"

"Alright, that's enough," said Belotsvetov in a conciliatory tone, "that's all we need now — a quarrel. Vasily's not a parachutist and you, Lev Borisovich, ought to be ashamed for getting pie-eyed at such an ungodly hour."

"Ashamed?" exclaimed Fondervyakin. "You should ask why it was I took a drink first thing in the morning before you shame me!"

"Alright then, why did you get pie-eyed at such an ungodly hour?"

"Because my personal beggary has finished me off once and for all! I'm not some parasite, I've slaved my whole life, like a horse, and what have I got to show for it? Practically nothing!"

"Just how do you mean, nothing?!" asked Vasily somewhat offended. "Your bank account has probably got incalculable thousands vegetating in it, so to speak, and here you are laying it on thick, like you're some beggar from Zagorsk!"

"We're not discussing my thousands right now. Right now we're discussing the fact that for thirty-five years of irreproachable service personal beggary instead of personal prosperity is my due. Have a look at how I live: a little divan, an armchair, and a television hardly better than an ancient KVN! It's getting to the point where I've got nowhere to stick sixteen jars of preserved apples! Thank God there are only fifteen now, so it's a bit easier . . ."

"Well, I've gotta run," interrupted Mitya, picking up his dishes. "You all carry on deliberating, but I've gotta run."

"After all, I'm not some Tuareg," continued Fondervyakin, as if emanating a sense of wounded pride. "For a Tuareg, utter poverty is a normal state, his heart doesn't bleed over having to sleep in a tent and ride around on a camel, because that's his nomadic lot. But Citizens, I'm a European, and maybe even more of a European than an Englishman and a Frenchman rolled into one, yet I live like a Tuareg! You've got to understand: I'm up to my ears, so to speak, in European sentiments and self-awareness, but the concrete reality is that I live in destitution. And naturally this infuriates me! In short, faced with a similar situation only a saint wouldn't get sloshed first thing in the morning, and I, Citizens, am no saint . . ."

That's the way life is: confused, lengthy, non-compositional, a multitude of extraneous components, which literature doesn't tolerate, but life does, since in life, for some reason, all is fish that comes to the net, and there is a reason why every little worm exists. Consequently, the description of the events that occurred on Saturday must in no way begin with the real-life quarrel that broke out in the kitchen first thing in the morning, but should conform instead to the innate demands of art.

Precisely so: for a time, Alexandra Sergeyevna's disappearance remained unnoticed, but by lunch Apartment 12 was already slightly intrigued as to why the old lady, who usually appeared in the common areas before the others, had not been seen by anyone all morning. This question had yet to ripen to the stage when questions escape the lips of their own accord: Vasily Chinarikov was still chipping away ice from under the gateway to building No. 2 as though nothing had happened; Belotsvetov was still lying imperturbably on his sofa, leafing through Kierkegaard's *Fear and Trembling*; Yuliya Golova was out shopping with Pyotr; Fondervyakin was stewing plum compote in the kitchen; Mitya and Lyuba were languishing at school; the Valenchiks were watching television; Anna Olegovna was tidying up her room. But a solemn, and for some reason partly pleasant uneasiness had already settled over the apartment.

Around three o'clock in the afternoon, when almost all of the tenants had crowded into the kitchen to attend to lunch-related chores, they started talking about Pumpianskaya's absence.

Fondervyakin asked himself aloud why Pumpianskaya was making herself scarce. Genrikh Valenchik presumed she'd gone out shopping, but Yuliya Golova rejected that presumption, saying it was impossible, for goodness sake, to traipse around the shops for four hours in a row. Then Belotsvetov proposed the following scenario: Pumpianskaya had suddenly gone to visit one of her relatives. Yet this scenario didn't withstand scrutiny either since Anna Olegovna announced that to her memory Pumpianskaya had never stayed away for more than an hour, and Fondervyakin testified that the last time the old woman had gone to visit relatives on the Arbat was in '48.

"Well, then she's died," said Lyuba Golova. "At best she's fallen sick."

And immediately a sinister silence ensued.

When the initial impact of these words evaporated, the men decided that someone ought to knock on Pumpianskaya's door. Chinarikov knocked, but there was no answer; Belotsvetov knocked — he didn't receive an answer either. Fondervyakin went up to the door, put his eye right up to the keyhole, and said:

"You can't see anything. The key must be sticking out from the other side."

"If the key's sticking out," announced Valenchik, "it means the old woman's home. Here's what you do, Vasily — sniff the keyhole, maybe it's already, you know . . ."

"But I smoke," answered Chinarikov. "I've got zero sense of smell. And corpses don't decompose in the first twenty-four hours, even in forty-degree heat."

"How would you know?" asked Fondervyakin.

"I just do . . . ," Vasily answered.

And again a sinister silence ensued, which betrayed not a sense of loss but one of acquisition.

"Yes," said Valenchik after a bit, "this business spells trouble! We ought to call the police."

Chinarikov hurried over to the telephone and started calling the housing office, an ambulance, and District Inspector Rybkin, with whom he was acquainted. The other tenants began dispersing to their own rooms, casting sidelong looks at Alexandra Sergeyevna's door as though it were already decided that a death had occurred behind it. Only Mitya Nachalov and Lyubov Golova lingered in the kitchen.

"Well, what do you think, sis? I suppose you're terrified," Mitya asked.

"Na-ah," said Lyubov.

"You're hard-hearted. I'm a guy, and it's even given me the willies."

"Here's what you'd better tell me, Mitka: does the phone call have anything to do with this?"

"Huh?"

"What's with you, got bananas in your ears? I said, does the phone call have anything to do with this?"

"Na-ah," answered Mitya, and he started to laugh. "Fondervyakin got drunk as a cobbler this morning — now that beats all . . ."

At a quarter to five the doorbell rang in the entrance hall and all of the tenants leaned out of their doorways. District Inspector Rybkin had arrived. He was a fine figure of a man, youthful for his age, who in lineups was surely called 'young man,' and by no means 'hey, mister,' as is the custom now due to the deterioration of polite forms of address. Of District Inspector Rybkin's traits, worthy of mention are his downy little mustache, reaching down to his lower lip in places, the fact that he always wore his service cap pushed back on his head, and the meekly tired expression of his eyes, which, by the way, also occasionally stared at you like the barrel of a gun.

"Well, what's the matter here?" asked Rybkin, folding his hands over his stomach.

"One of our tenants has disappeared," said Chinarikov. "Pumpianskaya, Alexandra Sergeyevna. She was still here yesterday, but today she's vanished as if by magic!"

"Aha!" said Rybkin, and he went down the corridor toward the kitchen.

While he was inspecting the door to Pumpianskaya's room, probing the doorknob and peeping into the keyhole, Fondervyakin gave him an account of how the old lady was unmarried, how the last time she'd gone to visit her relatives on the Arbat was in '48, and how she never absented herself from home for more than an hour. Then from a desire to ingratiate himself he even leaned against the left leaf of the door to show that this was an ancient door, solid, like a gateway.

At that moment, the doorbell rang in the entrance hall again. This time it was the building superintendent from the housing office, a sprightly girl by the name of Vostryakova, and one of the gloomy housing office locksmiths.

"Are we going to bust in?" Vostryakova asked Rybkin, in response to which the inspector nodded somewhat dolefully, though not right away — only after he'd removed his cap, wiped the inside of its crown with a handkerchief, and perched it once again on the back of his head.

The gloomy locksmith stepped up to the door with a collection of myriad keys, among which peeped out master keys, but he was unable to match anything and so had to resort to a jimmy. Rybkin watched the locksmith . . . not fraternally, it should be said.

Finally, the door emitted an unpleasant cracking sound and

opened, revealing an ever so dark rectangle reeking of close air. Everyone present at the unsealing of the room, namely the whole of Apartment 12, recoiled slightly. Having said, "I ask everyone to stay out . . . ," Rybkin fingered his holster mechanically and stepped over the threshold as into an abyss. He disappeared for a second, then the lights flashed on, and Apartment 12 clung to the door.

Pumpianskaya's room was vacant. Those who could get a peek saw a large sideboard of Karelian birch, an antique marble washstand with a mirror and pedal, a narrow metal frame bed, a nightstand, tailor-made to fit under a pot containing a dwarf pine, a large, round four-legged table covered, so it seemed, with a sheet, a landscape painting from another age, heaps of photographs in intricate frames, various dear articles such as a clock in a glass case, or candlesticks in the shape of hollowed-out eggs, or a long and narrow vase holding dyed feather grass — but the main thing was that those who could get a peek saw that Pumpianskaya's room was vacant.

"Comrades, why confuse the issue?" said Rybkin.

"Yes," agreed Fondervyakin, "it's certainly turned out badly. All we've done is to break into someone's lodgings as if it were a matter of course . . ."

"Meanwhile citizen Pumpianskaya," conjectured Anna Olegovna, "is probably riding the bus right now on the way to her second cousin's once removed on her mother's side and feeling wonderful, unlike us."

"Oh, but she hasn't got any second cousin," announced Genrikh Valenchik, "she hasn't got anyone at all. She was a solitary old woman, like a poplar in the steppe . . ."

"Why do you say 'was'?" asked Rybkin. "Do you . . . have precise knowledge that citizen Pumpianskaya no longer exists?"

Valenchik became confused and, having become confused, he uttered:

"No, I can't know that, of course. I only know that she hasn't got any relatives, not even of the type you'd call kissing cousins once removed. I even wonder whom she would've visited on the Arbat in her day."

"That's not even the point," stepped in Yuliya Golova, "at the end of the day, the point is that it's been twenty years since she left the house. Our old lady never budged, except to go down to the boulevard sometimes for a breath of fresh air."

"For twenty years she didn't go anywhere," said Lyuba, "and in the twenty-first she up and left!"

"How on earth could she have gone out if the room is locked from the inside?" Mitya objected.

"Good Lord!" exclaimed Vera Valenchik. "Surely Alexandra Sergeyevna wasn't kidnapped through the window?!"

"You should get out of here, Vera," said her spouse. "You're in no condition to get worked up."

Vera submissively made her way to their room. On the way she scooped up Pyotr who, having stuck his index finger in his mouth, had been following the adults' conversation so intently it seemed he understood absolutely everything.

"This affair is very simple to clear up," said the gloomy locksmith, and for some reason everyone was astonished by the fact that the locksmith had spoken. "The door in question has a patent lock, manufactured way back in the days of the NEP, no less. Slam it shut and it locks, and your old lady could've left the key on the inside out of forgetfulness."

"But all the same, it's suspicious somehow, if you know what I mean — unreal," said Fondervyakin, and he cupped his chin with his hand.

"First you should finish chewing . . . well, I don't know, whatever it is you're chewing," said Building Superintendent Vostryakova, turning to him, "and then engage in conversation."

"He's not chewing anything," explained Anna Olegovna, "that's just his pronunciation."

Fondervyakin turned crimson, and the expression on Vostryakova's face looked something like the kind women have when they exclaim: "For the love of God!"

"The fact remains," Mitya concluded, "that the old woman has disappeared, and disappeared Hitchcock-style at that, under the most mysterious circumstances."

"These are all conjectures," said Rybkin. "For the time being, Comrades, there are no grounds for panic. Once the allotted period of time has elapsed then we'll start panicking . . ."

Rybkin stammered on the word "panicking," because just then in the entrance hall the doorbell rang with a startling wickedness. Vasily Chinarikov rushed over to open up; one could hear the clanging of locks, then voices, then footsteps thundering in the corridor as if they owned the place, and the kitchen was invaded by three fine fellows in white smocks and short black greatcoats thrown over their shoulders à la Grushnitsky.

"Where's the body?" sternly asked the fellow in front.

"Well, there isn't any body exactly," responded Chinarikov, spreading out his hands to corroborate his words.

"What do you mean there isn't any body?" said the fellow in front with chagrin, bordering on disappointment. "Then why did you call an ambulance?"

Fondervyakin said to him crossly:

"Don't you worry about that, Comrades-in-medicine, I guarantee you, there will be a body!"

2

Night had already fallen, and in Apartment 12 all the lights were switched on when Belotsvetov led Inspector Rybkin out to the landing, touched his sleeve, and asked out of interest:

"Well, and what action do you intend to take?"

"Why, none," answered Rybkin simple-heartedly. "There's no evidence of a crime, not even of an incident. You're worrying for nothing, your little old lady will turn up — where is there for her to go? And if she doesn't turn up, then it probably means she's gone off someplace to die, like to Kozelsk. You know, there's no reason such a rash idea should not have occurred to her."

"Yes there is!" objected Belotsvetov. "Pumpianskaya had no intention at all of dying. She always conducted herself as if she had no intention of dying, as a matter of principle — we do have astonishing old ladies like that in this country."

"But some of your fellow tenants," said Rybkin, "are of a different opinion. For example, some have pointed out that only yesterday Pumpianskaya was complaining of ill health."

"Don't you believe them. The lot of them can hardly wait for her little room to be vacated, and for the sake of that little room they're capable of saying anything. They'd bury Pumpianskaya alive given half a chance. In a word, it's your call, but there's something fishy about this business. I'd stake my life on one of us being mixed up in this somehow, I can feel it, like rheumatics can bad weather!"

"As a matter of fact, the folks who've gathered here are anything but simple. For instance, one of them lodged a complaint against his neighbors today. And not just against any one of them in particular, but against all of them in one go. And not just a complaint, but a short poem."

"A denunciation in verse, was it?" asked Belotsvetov. "That's a new one, Comrade Rybkin. Well, what did the denouncer write?"

"Oh, all kinds of nonsense."

"There you go, that's even more evidence for you that our lot is capable of anything! It's your call, Comrade Rybkin, but some action ought to be taken."

"I'm not going to take any action, because practically nothing has happened yet."

"No disrespect, of course, but you know, it's irresponsible. A person has disappeared, don't you understand that?! We should be launching a nationwide search without delay, whereas you're engaging in sabotage!"

"If the police launched a nationwide search every time someone disappeared they'd have no time for upholding public order, investigating violations of the law, crime prevention — in other words, attending to their own immediate responsibilities. We have our hands full as it is with alimony defaulters, and here you want to stick us with a globetrotting old lady, too . . . !"

With these words Inspector Rybkin gave an exaggerated salute and began to mince down the stairs while Belotsvetov went back to the apartment and looked into Chinarikov's room, who wasn't in because, as before, he was hanging around the kitchen with

Fondervyakin, silently surveying the door that had already been sealed by Superintendent Vostryakova.

"Our lost soul will come home from some matinée," Fondervyakin was saying, "to find her room has been sealed. Won't that be fun!"

"Vasily," said Belotsvetov, "drop by my place for a minute."

Belotsvetov's room resembled the storeroom of a provincial library. Books and cardboard folders in a variety of colors were sitting on shelves, on a tiny writing table, directly on the floor, and even on the windowsill. A leather sofa, a few dirty glasses, and a large hunk of bread lying on volume three of a medical encyclopedia were the only indications that this was not an office but someone's abode.

"Well?" uttered Chinarikov, getting settled on the sofa.

"I only wanted to say," began Belotsvetov, sauntering around the room, "that Rybkin has flatly refused to search for Pumpianskaya."

"That was to be expected."

"Yes, but any idiot can see that Pumpianskaya hasn't just walked or ridden away, she's disappeared! Even Vera Valenchik, the epitome of simplicity itself, has grasped that this business couldn't have come about without there being criminal intent. What do you think of all this?"

"Here's what I think: there was an old lady and now she's all gone."

"Well, Vasily, I can't look at it that way! I just shudder to think that a terrible crime has been committed, and nobody gives a good goddamn."

"You're a difficult person, Nikita. You always have to make a big deal out of everything. Well, alright, but what if no crime has been committed, what if Pumpianskaya, say, checked herself into a hospital?"

"For a start, I'd phone around to all the hospitals! And when it turns out that she's not in any hospital — and that's precisely how it'll turn out, because I can feel a crime's been committed here, like rheumatics can bad weather — then permit me to look into your shameless eyes. No, Vasily, suit yourself, but this story is anything but simple. Remember, she received some kind of strange phone call yesterday, and then that stupid ghost appeared . . ."

"We can do without any of that, agreed?"

"Fair enough, but why was Fondervyakin drunk the next morning?"

"He was drunk because he felt like having a drink."

"You've got a pat answer for everything."

"And you've got an idiotic question for everything! You can't be like that, old boy, you've got to get a grip on yourself — I'd even say you've got to keep yourself in an *iron* grip."

"There's just one thing I can't understand. There are several million men and women in the Soviet Union who are furious because their lives have no meaning. To their misfortune, these people understand that there *should* be meaning, and they probably even look for it but never find it. And the meaning of life — here it is, right in the palm of our hand, and what's more, it's clear as day: the militant rejection of evil! No doubt it's difficult, even agonizing, not to waver, to uphold such a position — but for those willing, that is, for those who are enraged, it's a way out . . ."

"The meaning of life is a purely Russian fabrication. We fabricated it for the very same reason the Asians fabricated Buddhism: presumably from want of life's basic necessities. Look, eleven-twelfths of the globe's population have never heard of any kind of meaning of life whatsoever, and believe you me, they feel just fine!"

"I'll even agree to the one-twelfth. So then, for them the militant rejection of evil is the categorical way out of their situation, because in their respective positions each of them will to some extent be an Alexander the Great, and the world will submit to them, and for the following reason: because the vast majority of people do not commit evil — that is, they're able not to commit it — and because the militant rejection of evil is well within the capability of some part of the population. In addition to which I'll develop a pharmacological method for treating the evildoers so that before long evil and lethargy will inevitably be exterminated!"

"You're an idealist, Nikita, a inveterate idealist!"

"Okay then, what do you see that's idealistic in the pharmacological treatment of evildoers?"

"Don't even mention your idiotic pills! Not only is the idea funnier than perpetual motion, you'll get yourself into such trouble to boot you won't know what hit you. I think I told you the story about how a certain brilliant fellow was eaten alive by a scientific research institute: eaten alive, figuratively speaking, boots and all without even so much as a hiccup, and all because this fellow fulfilled the entire five-year scientific research plan single-handedly."

"No, you haven't told me that story."

"In that case, let me tell it to you . . ."

There was a knock on the door, then it opened partially, and Mitya's head showed through the crack.

"Nikita Ivanovich," said Mitya, "let's assemble a council."

"What's the matter?" asked Belotsvetov.

"A telegram has just arrived for our Pumpianskaya. I've already signed for it."

"What does it say?" exclaimed Chinarikov and Belotsvetov in unison.

"How in the world should I know? That's why I'm suggesting we assemble, to decide what to do with the telegram: do we open it or not?"

"Of course we open it!" Chinarikov announced.

Belotsvetov took the telegram from Dmitry, tore the paper trim holding the form together, unfolded it, and read: "I grieve over the dear departed. Zinaida."

"Holy smokes!" whispered Chinarikov.

"Things are going from bad to worse!" said Belotsvetov emotionally.

"A dodgy text," agreed Mitya, and he grew dark.

All three were silent for about a minute-and-a-half, and then Belotsvetov submitted a few hypotheses.

"I think," he said, "this telegram can be understood in three different ways. It's either a murderess mockingly informing us of a crime that's been committed, a mysterious witness alluding to a tragedy that has occurred before her very eyes, or some simple-hearted relative who's found out, by coincidence, about Pumpianskaya's death and was quick to express her condolences."

"But the real interesting part is: just who is this Zinaida?" Mitya added.

"That is shrouded in mystery," Belotsvetov replied.

"We have to suppose," Chinarikov began, "that it's unlikely we'll find satisfactory answers to all of these questions."

"And why not?" objected Belotsvetov. "All it would take is to go to the post office and use some plausible pretext to ascertain the address of whoever sent the telegram, and then we'll find out just who this Zinaida is."

This is what they decided: Mitya and Chinarikov would telephone the accident bureau and the hospitals, while Belotsvetov would head over to the post office and, if possible, ascertain the address of whoever sent the telegram.

This decision was made some time after six.

3

To depict the subsequent events of that Saturday in a way consistent with the laws of life, one would have to describe how Belotsvetov waited at the post office and then walked for a long time to the Nogina Square metro station, what sights he encountered along the way, what types of clothing and physiognomies caught his eye, and what he reflected upon along the way, that along the way he reflected in particular upon such superficial matters as the regularities of price fixing, which meant that strictly speaking he was not reflecting at all. Next, one would have to describe how he exchanged a fifteen-kopek piece for three five-kopek coins, went down an escalator, again observing clothing and physiognomies, how he then boarded a blue metro car, having remarked to himself that this had formerly been the color of the gendarmes and then, apropos, remembered the lines: "Farewell unwashed Russia, land of slaves, land of lords . . . ," how he rode in the metro car to the Avenue of the World station, whose eyes met his, whether he sat or stood, and if he stood, then was it in the aisle or in the corner, and which fragments of which conversations did he overhear in the meantime . . .

Literature, as has already been noted, loathes these details. It immediately grabs the bull by the horns, as the saying goes, sifting through reality beforehand and sweeping aside everything that doesn't correspond to some fundamental principle of its construction, in conformity with which it might also transform any activity, subject matter, or phrase. Literature, let's say, is unable to accept such an altogether real-life expression as: *Why are you breaking chairs, I'll never understand! Honestly, what a people: they come around and start breaking chairs right off the bat, as if that's why they'd been put there, so that anyone who felt like it could break them up for firewood. And it wouldn't occur to a single one of them that the chairs were funded from the public purse, meaning, that in breaking them up for firewood you were inflicting a loss upon your country. No, they come around and set about breaking chairs, as if there were nothing better to do . . .* Rather, literature will without fail wring out any excesses, thereby reducing the expression to the stance of a single character: " 'But why in the world break chairs, gentlemen, after all, it's a loss to the treasury!' shouted Porfiry Petrovich merrily." In other words, a certain rule comes into play whereby life is tamed, or perhaps complicated, to the level of literature, in the way a popular truth tames philosophical teachings, or perhaps complicates them, to the level of proverb.

Literature's fundamental principle of construction is elusive by nature in that it is rooted in artistic talent, and as has already been noted, this is an obscure value, one we may never puzzle out. So to discover even some of its particular virtues would already be an achievement, a minor victory. What first comes to mind: since literature carelessly hacks up and modifies objective reality however it pleases, based exclusively on the whims of artistic talent, then it follows that artistic talent is the particular ability to carelessly hack up and modify objective reality however the artist pleases. Thus it follows that anyone who brandishes a pen at life is already an artistic talent to one degree or another, even if he comes across like a small child who does his brandishing awkwardly and affectedly. Secondly, if taming life to the status of literature generally proves difficult, if life in its pure form carries over to the page only while kicking and screaming, then what's needed, simply, is to trim as many details as possible.

Therefore, we omit the details of Belotsvetov's adventures and grab the bull by the horns at the moment he walked into Vasily Chinarikov's room and said . . .

No, the room should be described first. Chinarikov's room was remarkable in that it contained a multitude of useful and beautiful objects that had been picked out of the garbage: a canapé with a quaint back and suspicious looking stains on the upholstery; a plaster-of-Paris bust of the poet Apukhtin; a few porcelain cups that had been neatly glued together, bearing portraits of Bonaparte's marshals; a bronze candelabra depicting the Three Graces holding torches; two mahogany chairs — one covered in leather and the other in a threadbare, blue damask; a detail of some sort — probably from an iconostasis — carved and covered in gilt, fixed to the wall; a card table with an inlaid wooden tabletop; a carpet, evidently valuable at one time, but completely moth-eaten now. On the walls, besides the detail from the iconostasis, hung a number of bookshelves completely crammed with the *Brockhaus and Efron Encyclopedia*, a piece of needlework framed under glass, and a full-length portrait of Ernest Hemingway.

Now then, Belotsvetov entered the room and said:

"Listen, Vasily, your patronymic doesn't happen to be Petrovich, does it?"

"Yes, it's Petrovich," said Vasily.

"Right! Excellent! Simply excellent!"

"What's so excellent?"

"Oh, nothing. Did you call around to the accident bureau and the hospitals?"

"I did. All day yesterday there were only four accidents in Moscow, and I even managed to find out what they were: a fellow was burnt to death as a result of his own careless smoking; a child was run over by a car; and two girls threw themselves out of windows. I would never have thought that so few flesh-and-blood fatalities could occur in such an enormous city. Our old lady isn't in any of the hospitals."

"That means it's still either a case of plain kidnapping, or kidnapping and murder."

"Looks like that's what it is. Well, and what can we congratulate you on?"

Belotsvetov looked Chinarikov in the eye very, very intently, and then told him, as if reluctantly, that at the post office they gave him the address of a certain Zinaida Nikitchina Kuznetsova, that she proved to be the god-daughter of the patriarch Sergei Vladimirovich Pumpiansky, the anniversary of whose death just happened to be yesterday, on which occasion Kuznetsova had sent his daughter a telegram, something she'd been doing diligently for the past forty years.

"So the notorious Zinaida," said Chinarikov, "has absolutely nothing to do with it. That's a pity."

"Why is it a pity?" asked Belotsvetov, somewhat wickedly.

"Because she was a thread, and now we're back at square one."

"Instead of a thread we've found a whole rope."

"For instance?" asked Chinarikov with a kind of nervous, or in any case heightened, curiosity.

"For instance . . ." Belotsvetov started to say, and then suddenly paused unkindly. "For instance, I've unearthed an Alexei Sarantsev, a great-nephew of our Pumpianskaya, and he's a most suspicious little fellow. Why . . . ? First off, he's the sole and, for lack of any other fish in the pond, so to speak, direct heir . . ." Belotsvetov paused again here and fastened his eyes upon Chinarikov's face, but it didn't betray anything. "Second, because he's unemployed, and an inheritance would come in very handy. Third, to my way of thinking he's quite the slyboots. Fourth, at one time he was interested in genealogy, which doesn't speak in his favor either. By the way . . . actually, forget 'by the way' — that's for later."

"So the notorious Zinaida is clean, then" said Chinarikov, pursuing his point.

"Yes, if we don't take into account that somehow she's too well-informed — suspiciously so — about what valuables are in Pumpianskaya's room. But that she's been sending Pumpianskaya telegrams of condolence for forty years is a fact."

"So, who remains under suspicion here?"

"Everyone!"

"What do you mean, everyone?"

"Just that — everyone," Belotsvetov told him, with a look of boredom. "Because each and every one of them stood to gain from Pumpianskaya's transit, as they say, to the other side."

"For instance?"

"For instance, Fondervyakin, Valenchik, and Kapitonova along with Mitya would gain from it because any freed-up living space is just what they'd want. I'd even put Petka Golova under suspicion since, for one, on the very night our old lady disappeared, he was sitting on a chamber pot in the middle of the kitchen for some reason, deliberately pretending to read the newspaper, and because he's capable of conscious villainy."

"Conscious villainy," objected Chinarikov, "is when the evil deed is profitable in some way, or at least not futile. What does Petka stand to gain by smearing your door handle with muck?"

"Right now, he doesn't stand to gain anything by playing dirty tricks on me, but the day after tomorrow he might — in other words, Petka's dirty trick on me might seem to have been transcendent, but maybe he did it with the most materialistic super-objective in mind. Even if we look at it your way, the upshot is senseless villainy, but that's even worse, isn't it, because it's more enigmatic, more incomprehensible. Although any evil is probably transcendent to some extent, because man emerged from nature, and there's never been any evil in nature."

"Of course there has!" exclaimed Chinarikov indignantly. "What about carnivorousness, and the law of the jungle, and the degeneration of species?"

"Well, what kind of evil is that? Natural, I would even say mechanistic, like death. That kind of evil does exist in nature, of course, and man inherited it, of course, but it just happens to be a necessary evil that, by means of the struggle of opposites, ensures eternal progression toward an ideal. But we're also aware of evil that is foreign to nature, unnatural, if you will, an evil invented by humankind, a sort of acquired evil! You'll agree that a raven wouldn't peck out the eyes of another raven, that God sends a curst cow short horns, that ultimately a lion — the king of the jungle — would never squeeze the life out of a lamb if his belly were full. But man would! Death, hunger, marital infidelities — these can be tolerated, they're normal, for they're inevitable and unavoidable, but denunciations, National Socialism, that business of the student Ivanov's murder by radicals — what would you have me attribute those to?! What I'm trying to say is that people have somehow incurred that same artificial, self-made evil, which is senseless to the point of being transcendent. Thus, like the bubonic plague or absolutist rule it can and should be eradicated."

"Your logic, Professor, is certainly weak, and its weakness is explained by your failure to begin at the beginning. To correct your first error: what's absent from nature is good, not evil, because in an architectonic sense good is non-constructive; so not only is there evil enough to spare, it is the kind of evil that is the most unnecessary, useless, ornamental even. Here are some examples for you: for no good reason whales beach on dry land; a genetic code can carry within itself a cancerous compound, even though it trends toward death anyway; ordinary pigeons, whose death even cabbies speak of in polite terms, suffer from terrible illnesses. Well okay, the cancerous compound, that's one thing, but why must pigeons get sick? To make a long story short, there's more senseless evil in nature than you can shake a stick at, while there's a complete absence of good, in principle, in the same way there are no Chinese hieroglyphics in the chemical formula for water . . . You know what, you should sit down — why are you standing there like you're rooted to the spot . . . ?"

Belotsvetov sat down in the leather armchair and said:

"Well, you're wrong. There *is* good in nature, only its scope is very narrow. Spencer even devised the concept of 'animal ethics,' which in higher mammals is expressed by their marking of territory, and the weaker male need merely be made to understand that he's weaker and he surrenders his female right off. Plainly, animal ethics and good, as perceived by the human mind, correspond to one another like the spinal cord and vertebral column."

"That's the whole point! These same Spencerian ethics are anti-ethics because they do nothing but further the law of the jungle. They constitute formal good, which provides impetus for completely non-formal evil, not unlike the way medieval justice condemned all kinds of witches, anatomists, practitioners of black magic and so on to burn at the stake from the best of motives.

"Now to your second error: it's *good* that's transcendent, not evil — evil just happens to be focused and comprehensible, and very much so at that. This follows, in part, from the fact that good is senseless from the individual's point of view, since in the best case it's futile and in the worst it's self-detrimental. Look, are we to assume that if a person chops off his hands so as not to be able to slap someone's face it is a transcendent act? Of course it is! Which is what required proving. But the way *you* see it, what requires proving is that evil is in the order of things, whereas good was invented by nomads from Judea."

"That's all fair enough, to a degree," agreed Belotsvetov, "but what you're not taking into account is that man came out of nature, like a chicken out of an egg — or more precisely, I should say man left nature, like the chicken left the egg. Hence this allegory: the egg is evil, and the chicken is what was invented by the nomads from Judea."

"I propose another allegory: if among wolves there were to appear a wolf so crazy that he ate hay in spite of himself, deliberately made friends with rabbits, and, out of melancholy made himself the willing target of a hunter's rifle, then that would be so-called *Homo sapiens*. Man is a particular, exalted form of nature's madness and nothing more."

"We've gotten somewhat confused," said Belotsvetov, slightly befuddled, and he passed his hand over his forehead. "Let's start over, from the top. Okay, so humankind grew out of nature — that doesn't seem to be in question."

"Not in question," agreed Chinarikov, albeit somewhat guardedly.

"But now here's a question: this being the case, is humankind the goal of nature, or is it the same accidental product of evolution, governed by the same laws of nature as everything else, animate or inanimate?"

"Ask me something easier," answered Chinarikov sadly, and he reached for a cigarette. "On the one hand, it would appear, of course, that man was programmed primordially somehow — in other words, if ultimately he came into being, it means he was programmed primordially. But on the other hand, it seems man is an accident of nature, or maybe some intermediate result, since it's doubtful that nature intentionally programmed such a dimwitted, even hostile creature who's capable of unceremoniously destroying nature itself — this, of course, is ridiculous."

"I'll take note of that intermediate result, but in the meantime allow me to state the following: The human race evidently developed not only programmatically but also supra-programmatically, so to speak, now proceeding, essentially, from itself. You see, let's assume that an ordinary German little Adolf was programmed in the Schickelgruber couple, but that what ultimately materialized was the historical man-eater. In a word, dimwittedness and the tendency toward self-destruction — that's still not a good enough argument. Nature might only have nurtured humankind up to a certain age and then ushered it out of the nest with a certain store of knowledge. Something else to consider is that if nature hatched humankind, why on earth was it so necessary for it to do so — why, eh?"

Chinarikov shrugged his shoulders lazily.

"Most likely man became necessary to nature," Belotsvetov started to answer himself, "because nature isn't conscious of its own existence, because man is nature's one and only mode of self-awareness."

"And what follows from this?"

"Who the hell knows what follows from this!" admitted Belotsvetov affably. He got up out of the armchair, sauntered back and forth across the room a few times, then settled on the sofa and crossed his legs. "Ultimately, nature simply found expression in human consciousness, and that's all there is to it. If we ever find the unambiguous 'because' to the question of 'why' nature did that, we'll pretty much have the answer to all questions. Although why, for example, was the ice age necessary for nature? Because it was, period! It's enough to know what's obvious to the intellect: that man is too strategic a result to have sprung from infusoria for no reason at all."

"Well, alright," said Chinarikov, releasing streams of blue-gray smoke through his nostrils. "Let's assume we've found the unequiv-ocal 'because' for your 'why'; let's assume we've decided that man — that is, ideal man — is the ultimate aim of nature. So where in the world are the answers to all questions? In general terms, how is all of this relevant to the struggle between good and evil?"

"Most directly!" said Belotsvetov resolutely. "If man is an accident of nature, he can't be held responsible, but if he's the ultimate aim of nature, then the question becomes why the hell is so much superfluous beastliness, crime, and mayhem so necessary to nature? And can it be true that two world wars, for example, were necessary to achieve perfection? Unless man really is a kind of intermediate result — not yet a human being in the strict sense but rather a Paranthropus. It could very well be that *Homo sapiens* is no more than a link, or a semi-finished product, if you like, while the end product, the one conceived by nature, is a kind of *Homo humanis* — in other words, a humane human, really something sublime, nothing less than unearthly. In short, the capricious circumstance whereby humankind at present consists primarily of swindlers and fools in no way refutes the supposition that man was conceived as a consummation, precisely as perfection. If he was conceived at all. Well, seeing as you and I are deciding: was he conceived or not?"

"Let's say he was," agreed Chinarikov reluctantly and sighed.

"And let's even say he wasn't conceived, let's even say humankind represents an evolutionary dead end — the whole thing is utter nonsense, because for the last two-thousand years man has been evolving not according to the laws of nature, but according to the laws of his species, proceeding from the idea of the individual. If, however, millions of thinking beings act unswervingly and expediently on some idea, be it the most artificial and absurd, then it becomes reality, a law of nature, a principle of evolution."

"What the hell is this idea of the individual now?" asked Chinarikov discontentedly.

"A very nebulous idea, see for yourself . . . First the wild beast or, better said, the proto-human, was armed against the world with only a certain knowledge, 'animal ethics,' and a mechanistic evil, which he neatly handed down along with his hairiness and fangs, because in the beginning, only evil ensured survival — in other words, food, security, and the female. But later on, the quantity of 'knowing' somehow developed into the quality of 'understanding,' and 'animal ethics' were somehow transformed into good. As for the parity of 'knowing' and 'understanding' — well, by now everything's more or less clear, if only because 'if you beat a rabbit long enough he'll learn to light matches.' But just how 'animal ethics' became the good — that's the big mystery. Although it may very well be that they became good by means of 'understanding.' After all, it wasn't such a stretch for the proto-human to understand that his survival was ensured not only by mechanistic evil, which nevertheless amounts to a kind of single-minded alienation, but also by good, or more precisely, a precursor to good, which amounts to a beneficial dealienation. Because not killing, not mutilating, not stealing your fellow man's last scrap is beneficial dealienation — in other words, something that also ensures survival, except without the effort, completely gratis. And that's roughly the way relative good could have split off from absolute evil."

"Now that, Professor, is already a kind of unbridled materialism," said Chinarikov, "and by the way, that's not the issue. The issue remains the same: what the hell is this idea of the individual?"

"I'm getting to it," answered Belotsvetov, putting up his hand in an obliging gesture. "So then, it looks as if evil is primary, like matter, and good is secondary, like consciousness, and not at all the other way around. Which is to say, that in the beginning it was primal evil and not the Word that provided grist for the mill of evolution — forgive the blasphemous turn of phrase. Which is to say, it wasn't the angel who sank down to the depths of the devil, but, in a manner of speaking, the devil who 'angelicized' himself. Which is to say, that having eaten from the Tree of Knowledge, Adam and Eve rose rather than fell, although their descendants paid a stiff price for that rising. Which is to say, Cain wasn't the first murderer, but Abel the first altruist, and an altruist of the most naive considerations at that, since he should've found himself a club to prevent Cain's murderous assault. But that's not the point right now; the point right now is that many thousands of years ago good somehow hatched out of evil.

"And now we come to the part shrouded in the most obscurity: the wild beast came to love good. Most probably he came to love it because every now and then he'd come to be its object. And having come to love good, our wild beast came to love himself, for in being the object of unconquerable evil it's only possible to loathe and feel contempt for yourself, whereas in being the object of good, *not* coming to love yourself is downright impossible. So right then and there man arose in the wild beast, or to be more precise, the individual did, since he who loves himself is conscious of himself in time and space, through which we, as such, distinguish ourselves from the other air-breathers of the world. Therefore, man is the child of good, as is that very same idea of the individual that guides the evolution of man: the idea of the individual as good . . ."

Toward the end of this monologue, that is, during the last couple of minutes or so, Chinarikov had begun scrutinizing Belotsvetov's right shoe, for which reason Belotsvetov was forced to break off what he was saying, and having broken off, he was silent for a moment, then asked:

"Hey, Vas, why are you looking at my shoes?"

Chinarikov answered: "You've got a hole in your right shoe."

"Where?" asked Belotsvetov, taking such a lively interest it turned comical when he also began to scrutinize his shoe.

"Not there, on the sole," Chinarikov prompted him, "in the toe."

"A hole indeed," pronounced Belotsvetov, picking at it with his finger, and then he continued: "Well, so there it is. It ended by nature generating a twofold creature, so to speak. On the one hand, this creature was the bearer of rational evil, which he inherited from the wild beast, but he also bore good — a yet unknown quality that transcended the limits of nature and had hatched out of evil for the sole reason that orthograde man had begun to acquire comprehension. This is where it all began! Given the dichotomy that was generated in this entirely new level of qualities, further development subsequently proceeded on a completely different plane as well — that of human life and the history of humankind, which is to say, that's where it all began: indulgence, self-sacrifice, wars, Tolstoyism, National Socialism, marital infidelities. But this is understandable, not least because man and mankind have been endowed with the potential for everything, because I can pick up a stray kitten on the street today and steal a broom from my neighbor tomorrow, because the vast majority of people are neither good nor evil in absolute terms, but both not-so-good and not-so-evil at the same time."

"Listen, Professor," Chinarikov interrupted him, "isn't it our bedtime . . . ?"

"Hang on a minute with your bedtime! You should have a look instead at the kind of nonsense this produces. If man is the bearer of rational evil, then what is it that compels him to smear door handles with muck?!"

"Here we go again!" said Chinarikov in lazy exasperation.

"No, most likely the transcendent villain is nothing more than a madman after all, and he ought to be given the same medical treatment as your garden-variety psychopath."

At these words, there was a knock on Chinarikov's door.

Chinarikov and Belotsvetov exchanged glances, as though asking one another who it could be at such a late hour, after which Vasily said, "Come in." The door opened and District Inspector Rybkin appeared on the threshold. For some reason his appearance produced such a powerful effect on Chinarikov that he got up from behind the table so abruptly he knocked a metal vase containing water and a desiccated branch of willow herb onto the floor.

"Well, what about it, Comrades," said Rybkin, "are you satisfied now that nothing should be done in haste save gripping a flea?"

"I don't get it," said Belotsvetov somberly.

"What exactly is there to get? Your old lady's been found. Here you were getting hysterical on me, and she's turned up."

"Oh boy!" exclaimed Chinarikov. "We didn't know what to think anymore. Thank you, Comrade Rybkin, for such welcome news . . ."

"Wait, wait," Rybkin stopped him. "Do you mean you haven't seen citizen Pumpianskaya with your own eyes today?"

"No, we haven't," said Belotsvetov. "What makes you think our old dame has turned up in the first place?"

"Oh boy!" uttered Rybkin now, too. "I'm going up the backstairs around ten — to Apartment 22 because another fight had broken out there — and suddenly I see that the light's on in Pumpianskaya's room . . . ! Well, so I thought the old lady'd been found, and that some comrades had been getting hysterical for nothing."

"Come to think of it, why are we guessing if the old lady's turned up or not . . ." said Chinarikov. "Let's go see for ourselves!"

All three went out into the corridor, filling the drowsy apartment with the disturbing din of footsteps. Arriving in the kitchen, they stopped opposite Pumpianskaya's room, which the sprightly Vostryakova had recently sealed off. The stamped seal was in place.

"Hmm," mumbled Rybkin pensively.

He then picked the seal off and pushed one side of the door open. A dark quadrangle of air was visible, and it was already giving off the odor of something deathly — in any case, uninhabited.

"Praise thy wonders, O Lord!," remarked Chinarikov. "None other than the ghost has visited us again."

"As for the ghost, just drop it," said Rybkin edifyingly. "I mean, what subjective idealism . . . !"

With these words he stepped into Pumpianskaya's room, switched on the light, and looked around attentively. Everything here was as before, and nothing seemed to indicate an intruder. In fact, it seemed as if no one had inhabited Pumpianskaya's room for a long time.

"Listen, Lieutenant," said Belotsvetov, "is there any chance you could have made a mistake?"

"I'm not at liberty to slip up for no reason at all," answered Rybkin. "Otherwise I'm not worth a damn."

"Get a load of this, Comrades!" exclaimed Chinarikov suddenly, jabbing his finger at the floor. "A footprint!"

Indeed, some twenty to thirty centimeters from the threshold there was the vague impression of a shoeprint.

"It's possible that someone left it last time," suggested Rybkin wanly.

"Very possible," agreed Chinarikov, and he looked Belotsvetov piercingly in the eye, the way people do when they're about to incriminate someone.

"To tell you the truth, I don't like this at all," said Rybkin with a somewhat unkindly expression on his face.

"And what could be good about it?" confirmed Belotsvetov. "Without rhyme or reason an elderly woman disappears, and what's more, she disappears under sufficiently mysterious circumstances . . ."

"For instance?" asked Rybkin.

"For instance, on the eve of Pumpianskaya's disappearance someone telephoned her but decided to clam up. For instance, that night Petka Golova was sitting in the dark kitchen on a chamber pot, deliberately pretending to read the newspaper. For instance, the morning after Pumpianskaya's disappearance our neighbor Fondervyakin was as drunk as a cobbler, and afterward he told the boys from the ambulance service that the affair would definitely produce a corpse. All in all it paints a nasty picture."

All three fell silent, as though deep in thought.

"Hello, boys!" suddenly rang out a voice behind them, and the posse turned around.

It was Lev Borisovich Fondervyakin standing in the middle of the kitchen, wrapped in a striped sheet.

"What've you all crowded in here to peep at so late?" At these words Fondervyakin playfully bowed his head, and his bald patch began to shine like a newly minted five-kopek coin.

No one answered him.

"Here's what I think," Fondervyakin began to say. "None of this is as simple as it might seem at first glance. Most likely there's some age-old story here: collaboration with the Nazis, or even a link to a foreign spy mission now liquidating its agents . . ."

"Shame on you, you old coot," responded Chinarikov. "What are you going on about — it's beyond comprehension! Next you'll be saying Pumpianskaya had connections to the spirit world!"

"You bet I will! It's no coincidence that Yulka Golova saw a ghost!"

In someone's room a radio sounded midnight, ringing in Sunday.

SUNDAY

1

At six o'clock in the morning, Fondervyakin peeped into the kitchen, hoping to have a chat with somebody about the second coming of the ghost, but the kitchen was deserted, so he went off to get some more sleep.

At around eight, when outside the day was only just beginning to dawn and Apartment 12 was still dreaming light Sunday dreams, Vasily Chinarikov dropped into Belotsvetov's room, took a seat on the edge of the couch, jabbed him in the side with his fist and said:

"Let's have a candid talk."

Long awake, Belotsvetov opened his eyes.

Puffing away on one of the crude cigarettes he seemed forever to have in his mouth, Chinarikov filled the room with a mass of smoke that looked white as steam in the gloom. Usually nonchalant, he gave off an unpleasant aura of tension.

"What were you doing in Pumpianskaya's room yesterday?" he asked.

"How do you know I was there?"

"Alright, don't play the fool . . ."

"No, really, how?"

Chinarikov sighed complacently:

"It was easy to figure out. Remember when Rybkin came here

yesterday, and I accidentally knocked over the vase with the willow herb in it?"

"Well yes, I do."

"A puddle formed on the floor, and you stepped in it."

"So what?"

"Here's what: your wet shoeprint and the dry shoeprint we found in Pumpianskaya's room were made by one and the same shoe. In both cases the hole in the right shoe left an imprint — that is, it didn't leave an imprint, and that's what gave you away. Now, tell me what you were doing in the old woman's room."

"Whatever I was doing, I'm innocent as a babe in arms," said Belotsvetov with dignity. "But you, Vasily, I cannot vouch for."

"And why not?"

"Because you're a Petrovich!"

"Well, how do you like that . . . ! You must not be awake yet, Professor."

Belotsvetov sat up, lowered his bare feet onto the floor, groped around for his slippers, got up, walked over to the window, adjusting his satin shorts — in a word, he deliberately behaved in a way that would convince Chinarikov he had indeed woken up. Then he said:

"If I didn't know you inside out — if I didn't know you were a fully sound and decent person — I wouldn't even give you the time of day. But seeing as I do know this, I'm giving you a chance either to repent or to vindicate yourself in some way. And now, brace yourself . . ."

Chinarikov pricked up his ears — it could even be said he took fright.

"Yesterday I found out that you, Vasily, are an indirect heir of our old woman. You're a distant relative of hers, Citizen Chinarikov, and just you try to say this is news to you!"

"It *is* news to me!" said Chinarikov, somewhat unsteadily. "It's more than news, you've completely bowled me over, Nikita!"

For two or three seconds Belotsvetov stared Chinarikov in the eyes so intently it seemed he was seeking out their crystalline lenses.

"What do you want from me?!" implored Chinarikov. "I really didn't know Pumpianskaya was my relation!"

"Swear to it!" said Belotsvetov gravely.

"I swear . . ."

"No, swear on something!"

"Alright," agreed Chinarikov, his face becoming somewhat drawn, "I swear on the blood spilled at Kandahar."

Belotsvetov cast down his eyes and said:

"I believe you."

Some time passed in awkward silence, so to ease the excess tension Belotsvetov began to get dressed. Having made himself presentable, as the saying goes, he declared the following:

"As for me, I ought to inform you that I sneaked into Pumpianskaya's room in order to ascertain if Kuznetsova really has been sending our old lady telegrams of condolence for forty years. And just my damned luck, Rybkin had to end up on our floor right then!"

"That's fine," responded Chinarikov, "but you'd better tell me how you found out that Pumpianskaya and I are related."

"Remember my telling you recently about Alexei Sarantsev, who's busy studying his family tree? Well, he revealed to me that from his great-great-grandmother Verzhbitskaya and some descendant of Minister of War Milyutin there extended a branch that Sarantsev lost track of to a Pyotr Vasilyevich Chinarikov — very likely your father."

"My sainted aunt!" exclaimed Chinarikov. "So that means I'm even a noble to boot."

"What an idea!" said Belotsvetov. "Far more interesting is that it looks like we're all related by blood, and even a couple times over apiece. True, the idea's an ancient one, and it's been chewed over again and again you might even say, but still, it's marvelous to think that some shrew sitting behind the till isn't actually a shrew at all but your third cousin!"

"That's bad Nikita, oh it's bad!" said Chinarikov, shaking his head.

"What are you talking about?"

"What I'm talking about is that Alexandra Sergeyevna might be my fourth cousin once removed, and I haven't said a neighborly word to her the whole time . . ."

"You're right," Belotsvetov agreed with him, "that is bad."

"If the old lady really was done in, I won't rest until I find the culprit and tear his head off with my own hands!"

"Only first we have to find him," said Belotsvetov with a wide-eyed stare. "In the meantime we haven't got a single lead to go on."

"What do you mean we don't? Was there a secret phone call? There was. Did Fondervyakin promise a dead body? He did. Did somebody drop in on us on the eve of Alexandra Sergeyevna's disappearance? Someone did! And you're saying there isn't a single lead . . ."

"I can add one more, although again, it's highly speculative. The first thing I found in Pumpianskaya's room were the forty telegrams of condolence for her late lamented father in the sideboard drawer, but then I noticed something very strange: to the right of the sideboard, in the place where Pumpianskaya's wall is covered in photographs, gaped an empty space — it absolutely gaped — that is, among the photographs the small square of fresh, unfaded wallpaper stood out. What does this suggest? It suggests that a photograph has been swiped."

"Hmm!" mumbled Chinarikov and clapped a hand over his lower jaw.

"What was in the photograph? who could've wanted it? was it swiped before or after Pumpianskaya's disappearance? — these questions, of course, remain unanswered."

"It'd be tempting at least to find out what was in the photograph though."

"I agree," said Belotsvetov.

"Suit yourself, but my intuition tells me this photograph is at the crux of the matter."

"We've got to keep it in mind in any case. Except here's the pickle we're in: not all of our leads add up. Let's recall how events have unfolded: on Friday morning Pumpianskaya complained about her health, then someone telephoned her, but clammed up, then Yuliya Golova saw that idiotic ghost and got the whole apartment worked up . . ."

"What's more," Chinarikov put in, " Alexandra Sergeyevna showed up in the corridor a little later and asked what was the matter, to which Mitya replied, 'A ghost appeared.' "

"And about ten minutes before that," continued Belotsvetov, "I stopped by the kitchen and caught Petka Golova sitting on a chamber pot, pretending to read the newspaper."

"Incidentally, isn't there some sort of link between the appearance of the ghost and Petka sitting on the chamber pot?"

"I doubt it. We're going to have to talk to Petka, though. Right . . . and what happened next?

Yuliya saw the ghost . . ."

"We're going to have to talk to her, too," put in Chinarikov.

"Absolutely. She saw the ghost, screamed, and our whole anthill poured into the corridor."

"Lastly, Alexandra Sergeyevna went out to switch off the lights — I heard that with my own ears."

"Is that it?"

"That's it . . ."

Belotsvetov paced broodingly from the window to the door twice, then stopped in the middle of the room, pinched the bridge of his nose, and said:

"None of this makes any sense! It's as though Pumpianskaya has simply disappeared into thin air! I don't know about you, Vasily, but I can't come up with any scenario."

"What if it was like this: one of our tenants bumped off Alexandra Sergeyevna in the middle of the night, quietly removed the body and buried it somewhere . . . ? Then the only thing left to figure out is which one of us is capable of such a thing and it's case closed."

"And the phone call? It's as clear as day that someone was checking to see if Pumpianskaya was home."

"Alright. Some outsider got into the apartment in the middle of the night, bumped Alexandra Sergeyevna off, removed the body and buried it somewhere."

"And the ghost? How does the ghost fit in?"

"Well, maybe the ghost has nothing to do with it. After all, it appeared to Yulka alone and, well, did it appear or is Yulka just plain crazy? — that's an open question. In a nutshell, Professor, there's only one course of action left for you and me: we figure out which of us tenants, and which of the outsiders we know, is capable of such a murderous act, and then we squeeze a confession out of him."

"That's impossible for two reasons. First, the only outsiders we know of are Sarantsev and Kuznetsova, but there might be some Ivan Ivanovich Dushkin out there who bumped our old lady off. Second, in theory everyone is capable of such a murderous act. Heaven knows I'm a harmless enough creature, yet sometimes even I can feel the potential for murder inside me, so to speak. And the thoughts that cross my mind at times . . . ! If you knew what kind of thoughts cross my mind at times, Vasily, you'd even stop greeting me."

"Thoughts are one thing, deeds quite another," pronounced Chinarikov, embarrassed at the triteness of his words.

"But the point is that there is a beast crouching in all of us — oh, is there ever!"

"Well, I don't know," said Chinarikov. "After having been 'across the river' and had a good look at war — the way these things go — I can't even swat a fly. Because, Nikita, I've seen things no man's supposed to see when times are good."

"True, in one person the beast crouches, ready to pounce, in another it just loiters, while in someone else only its spirit has remained. Though it's exceptionally rare for a savage spirit not to be found in a healthy body, and that's how it should be, because we were born of fauna, and of flora, and two million years is not time enough for a godlike being to develop from paramecium infusoria. In time the savage spirit inside us surely will disappear, but the present generation of Soviet people won't live to see that red-letter day, not by a long shot."

"You're a lucky man, Nikita," said Chinarikov, sighing slowly. "Just two steps away from you they're maliciously disposing of innocent old ladies, just three steps from the Kremlin you can run into a beaten-up woman wearing a pair of mismatched boots, on the other side of that wall there lives a young Neanderthal in the person of Mitka Nachalov, and here you're expounding optimistic theories . . ."

"Where do you get that Mitka's a Neanderthal? Have you ever once spoken with him heart-to-heart?"

"I've got nothing to say to him," grumbled Chinarikov, "he's got nothing but nonsense on his mind."

"How do we know what he's got on his mind? What if he just happens to have Marxist-Leninist philosophy on his mind?"

Chinarikov smiled wickedly and suggested:

"That's easy enough to check. Let's go over to his room and ask: 'Hey there, Dmitry, how about telling us what's on your mind, boy?'"

"I don't see anything ironic in that question."

"Well then, let's go, what are you waiting for?!"

Belotsvetov's face betrayed a moment's hesitancy, but the very next instant he nodded in agreement, and they walked out of the room and into the corridor.

Since Pumpianskaya had looked after the electricity in Apartment 12 from time immemorial, none of the tenants had gotten around to turning on the lights, and the corridor was as dark as a winter morning. Near the front door, closer to the antique mirror, stood a shape, perceptible enough in the semi-darkness because it was much darker.

Seeing the shape, Chinarikov and Belotsvetov were struck dumb, and they both froze in awkward poses. About half a minute passed before Chinarikov got a grip on himself and asked in a voice not quite his own:

"Just who might you be, Comrade . . . ?"

"Me?" repeated the shape as terrestrially as could be. "Well, let's assume I'm Dushkin, Ivan Ivanovich. Are there any other questions?"

Chinarikov answered: "There are."

2

At about the time Belotsvetov and Chinarikov arrived at the idea of panhuman kinship, Apartment 12 was beginning little by little to awaken. The swooshing of water began in the bathroom and toilet; dishes started to clink cheerfully in the kitchen; footsteps, coughing, and the creaking of doors were heard. When on the Pokrovsky side the sun rose over the lopsided roofs and hit the windows with light of the same tender rosy hue found on Russula caps, already present in the kitchen were Lev Borisovich Fondervyakin, settled by the window and drinking milk from a dark blue mug with a gold rim, which for some reason he called a "goblet," Genrikh Valenchik, pressing together the edges of some special sort of *pelmeni*, Vera Valenchik, supervising him, Anna Olegovna Kapitonova, frying eggs on the stove, Mitya Nachalov, doing absolutely nothing, and Yuliya Golova, sitting on the stool, smoking.

Out of the blue, Fondervyakin said:

"The ex-world chess champion Anatoly Karpov is a stamp collector."

"So, what of it?" asked Yuliya Golova.

"Nothing. Just that he's a stamp collector."

"I'm going to speak frankly," said Valenchik, entering into the conversation. "If you ask me, stamp collecting and chess are one and the same thing. What do I mean by that? I mean that from the humanistic point of view, being the world chess champion is the same as being the world champion at standing on one's head. And they fuss over him like I don't know what — like the French over Napoleon. Let's say Rooster is also an interesting game, but can you imagine a world champion at Rooster who would be fussed over like the French over Napoleon?"

"All the same, Genrikh, you're a strange one," proclaimed Fondervyakin. "Chess isn't just a game, it's an intellectual art, so to speak."

"I would ask that you not broach the realm of art," said Valenchik nervously.

"For God's sake, Genrikh, don't get yourself so worked up," said Vera. "Your face is a sight to behold."

"Well, why wouldn't it be?" Mitya chimed in. "It's even more than that — not just a face, but an iconic countenance. Genrikh Ivanovich, when you're angry your face becomes downright regal."

Genrikh Valenchik relaxed and said:

"You know, Dmitry, sometimes I also think that I've got an unusual face, different somehow, especially compared to the physiognomies of the old regime, so to speak, back in the days of tsarist minting. Just yesterday I saw a photograph Petka had of some antediluvian fellow — well, an oligophrenic compared to me, an absolute oligophrenic!"

"Wait a minute, Genrikh Ivanovich," said Mitya keenly, "what photograph are you talking about?"

"To repeat, an ordinary photograph of a fellow in uniform with a physiognomy that's just asking for it, as the saying goes. It'd even been torn into four pieces and clumsily taped back together . . ."

At that very moment Chinarikov and Belotsvetov saw the shape in the dark entrance hall.

"How did you get in here, Vanya?" Chinarikov asked the interloper.

"Well, I *am* a first-rate locksmith," he answered slyly, "opening any door is a piece of cake for me."

Belotsvetov's vision had already adapted somewhat to the darkness, and he recognized the locksmith from the previous day, the one who'd forced open Pumpianskaya's door.

"I rang your doorbell again and again — not a single person opened up!" added the locksmith, "so I had to put my particular expertise to use."

"How many times did you ring?" asked Chinarikov, nodding significantly to Belotsvetov.

"Twenty-four times, three rings each."

"It stands to reason, then. Three rings — that's Pumpianskaya's code. The others wouldn't react to three rings any more than they would to ultrasound."

"We'll keep that in mind. Well, I'm off to inspect the vacant room."

"On what grounds?" Belotsvetov stopped him short.

"Officially, there are none, but if I like the room, Comrades, I'll be staying for a while. Are there any other questions?"

Belotsvetov and Chinarikov said nothing as the locksmith walked indifferently between them and disappeared around the corner.

"This is extraordinary, so help me!" whispered Belotsvetov in a single breath. "How I had this locksmith pegged, I'll never understand! Not half an hour ago I remember saying: 'Maybe there's some Ivan Ivanovich Dushkin who's bumped off our old lady!' You're a fine one, too. Why didn't you inform me there was a locksmith by that name in your housing office?"

"I had no idea he was Dushkin, Ivan Ivanovich! We've only ever called him Vanya-the-locksmith, and Vanya-the-locksmith . . ."

"Well, I am quite the seer!" said Belotsvetov, his eyes glittering. "I really hit the bull's eye! And I'll tell you something else: he's the one who bumped off our old lady. He jimmied the front door, got into Alexandra Sergeyevna's room, crowned her with something, and dragged her away down the backstairs . . ."

"Except that evening he came twice," Chinarikov corrected him. "First he bumped into Yulka and probably took to his heels, then showed up again a little later."

"All told, if Yuliya was able to make him out and her description corresponds with Dushkin's distinctive features, then it means he's the one who killed Pumpianskaya . . . !"

"Well then, the only thing left to do is to go to Yulka and question her about everything."

"Come on," Belotsvetov said.

Chinarikov rapped on Yuliya Golova's door with his index finger. They weren't invited in, but they entered anyway.

The room was contemporary in décor, with an enormous rug taking up almost the entire side wall, a floor lamp with a silk shade, two low armchairs on castors, the type of "unyielding" furniture that is somewhat inhuman, office-like — too geometric in any case. They didn't find Yuliya in, but they did find the apartment's youth. Pyotr Golova, looking up from under his brow, was tied to a table leg with some string. For some reason there was a light terry towel hanging around his neck. Opposite him, their backs to the door, Lyubov and Mitya were sitting in the chairs.

"A regular Red Banner upbringing," Mitya was saying.

"And who would've expected it?" echoed Lyubov. "Hey you, what's the matter, cat got your tongue? Answer when your elders address you!"

Pyotr was piously silent.

"What is it you're doing here, kids?" Belotsvetov inquired.

Mitya and Lyubov turned around at the sound of his voice and smiled identically.

"They're torturing me," explained Pyotr angrily.

Chinarikov asked to be shown the exact method being used, and Mitya readily demonstrated. He gagged Pyotr with the towel, and immediately the little boy's eyes bugged out.

"It's called 'air rationing,' " commented Lyubov.

"Not bad, these games of yours!" muttered Chinarikov, nodding his head somewhat broodingly.

"Listen, Vasily," said Belotsvetov, "you and I were going to pick Dmitry's brains about something."

"We were going to ask him what he had on his mind."

"Exactly. Hey, Dmitry, how about telling us what's on your mind, boy?"

The question did not sit well with Mitya Nachalov. His face grew pinched, his mouth tightened, his eyes seemed about to blaze, but then at once began to extinguish.

Chinarikov made an attempt to answer for him:

"Judging by your pastime, it sure isn't Marxist-Leninist philosophy."

"How so?" retorted Mitya. "I share our theoretical perspective. Theoretically, I agree entirely that profiting from someone else's labor is a disgrace, that being determines consciousness, that the construction of a communist society is a question of time, that the world is knowable, and there is no God."

"All's well in theory. But where do we stand in practice?" Belotsvetov said.

"In practice it's like this," answered Mitya, drawling. "Life is one thing, and philosophy — quite another."

"And you, Mitya, are a cynic!" said Chinarikov with feeling.

"I'm not a cynic, it's just that I've got a sober outlook on things."

"Wait a minute, Dmitry," Belotsvetov started to say. "What about Great Russian Literature? Is it also just . . . quite another thing?"

"Reading Great Russian Literature, Nikita Ivanovich, does more harm than good, especially at the start of one's journey through life."

"What a thing to say!" exclaimed Belotsvetov in amazement.

"You see, here's the thing," said Mitya pensively, "Great Russian Literature is the great deceiver of youth because it encourages and mobilizes us for the kind of life that simply can't exist. The reality is, if I live by the example of, say, Pierre Bezukhov, then before long I'll have nothing to eat."

"Right . . ." Belotsvetov managed to articulate. "You don't have a very high opinion of our life, Dmitry."

"Not so," said Mitya, somewhat reluctantly, "it's a regular life, like any other . . ."

"You just haven't cottoned on to it yet," Chinarikov observed.

"Exactly," corroborated Belotsvetov. "This deplorable state of affairs that finds the honor and conscience of the Russia of old on the brink of extinction, like Steller's sea cow, is a fact of life, as the saying goes. Nonetheless, dear Mitya, ours is such an amazing land, that sometimes you can't take a step without bumping into a Pierre Bezukhov. I don't know why things have turned out that way here, but this is also a fact — a restorative, invigorating fact. And perhaps the greatest enigma is that our lives here are beautiful filth or, if you like, agonizing delight. In other words, on the one hand it seems that all the chance misfortunes, scoundrels, and imbeciles have made living impossible, when in fact, lo and behold, on the other side of the wall, somebody's dreaming up a theory of universal prosperity, somebody's sending his last pair of trousers to a region struck by natural disaster, somebody's crying over poetry, or else a beautiful woman simply walks up to you and says: 'My darling, near and dear one, what is your wish? I'll hang myself, if you like — would that please you?' "

"Nikita Ivanovich, I don't know where you run into Pierre Bezukhovs," said Mitya, "more and more often I come across Yudushka Golovlevs. But I give you my word of honor, show me one saint, show me one noble deed, and I'll convert to your eccentric beliefs. Only you won't show me anything, because there's nothing to show. Why look afar? Standing right here is Vaska Chinarikov, a real piece of work, doesn't let a single skirt pass him by. Not a single skirt gets by you, does it, Vas, not even the pregnant ones put you off — you've even been cozying up to Lyubka, haven't you?"

Lyubov pressed her lips together tightly and turned away, her expression showing everyone that this was true, while Chinarikov bristled and uttered:

"You're still a bit young to be chastising me . . ."

Pyotr was picking his ear, as before, but this was a subterfuge. In actual fact he was listening avidly to the conversation.

"Okay, Mitya, it's a deal," said Belotsvetov. "I don't know about a saint, but I guarantee you a deed. It pains me, Mitya, that you don't believe in our literature and turn a cold shoulder to our way of living. For the sake of returning you to the fold, I'll forfeit my last bit of health, if you're interested in knowing, but I will save your soul. Just understand one elementary thing: you're hostile to our way of life because you simply do not understand it. And you do not understand it partly because you don't believe in Great Russian Literature. You think it's just fairy tales, but it's not fairy tales at all, dear Mitya, it's Russian life as it really is — it's just that life in this country is truly a little fantastic. Here's proof for you: in real life and real literature everything is held up by truth, conscience, and love."

Mitya smiled condescendingly and subtly winked at Lyuba.

Lyuba said, "But my mom says the main thing in life is knowing the lay of the land."

"By the way," said Chinarikov, "where is your blessed mommy?"

"She's at the housing office," answered Pyotr for his sister. "They've got some kind of hobby club. Cutting and sewing, or something . . ."

Chinarikov and Belotsvetov exchanged glances and left. In the entrance hall Belotsvetov took Chinarikov by the sleeve and said:

"You know what's just occurred to me? That possibly for the first time in the entire history of the Russian people a generation has emerged in this country who have no moral compass whatsoever, who simply do not know the difference between good and bad, between what must be done and what must not."

Chinarikov kept silent.

"It's as though something's happened to time and they're the first ones on Earth. The Bible, Christ, Roman law, Spinoza, the Encyclopedists, 'Liberty, Equality, Fraternity' — all this still lies ahead . . ."

"Didn't I tell you Mitka Nachalov was a Neanderthal?"

"You're a fine one, too, by the looks of it! Is it really true you've set your sights on Lyubov, you old lecher?"

"What can I do about it? Can I help it if I have liquid electricity running through my veins instead of blood?!"

3

The housing office occupied a few adjacent rooms on the first floor. In contrast to the St. Petersburg variant, where "the stairway was very narrow, steep and covered in slops. All the kitchens of all the apartments on all four floors opened onto the stairway and remained open for almost the whole day . . . ," this staircase was very decent and, it stands to reason, there were no kitchens at all. To make up for it, though, the "stuffiness was overwhelming, and the nauseating smell of fresh, wet paint and rancid drying oil from the newly painted rooms assailed his nostrils."

Belotsvetov knocked on one door, then another, and finally found what he was looking for. In a smallish room with bare walls, behind little tables resembling school desks, a company of women was holding a meeting; each woman had the same languid expression frozen on her face. At first Belotsvetov's glance fell upon an old woman in glasses, then upon a young woman in corduroy jeans, then upon some sort of rabbit-fur coat, and only after that did he see Yuliya Golova. He nodded to her, and she smiled apprehensively.

"Well it's about time at least one man came to join us," said an unfamiliar lady in a gray jacket, as slim and pale as a stearin candle. "Have a seat, Comrade!"

Embarrassed, Belotsvetov sat down on a free chair.

"Therefore, friends," the lady continued, addressing everyone now, "the Merezhkovsky-Gippius-Filosofov triangle was an unusual one. What united it was more than lust and passion — which were extinguished, by the way, during the period of reaction from 1907–09 and the economic boom that followed — it was also united by common aesthetic and sociopolitical perspectives." That's all for today. Next time we'll examine the Blok-Mendeleyeva-Bely triangle."

Chairs thundered, and the room emptied out in one minute. In the corridor Yuliya Golova walked up to Belotsvetov and asked:

"Has something happened?"

"Oh, no," said Belotsvetov. "Nothing's happened, I don't think. I just wanted to talk to you about the ghost."

"Ah-h," drawled Yuliya, either with disappointment or relief.

"By the way, that's a strange club you're in," observed Belotsvetov.

"There's nothing strange about it, it's a club like any other."

"Well, it's just that I didn't understand what the discussion was about."

"Great love triangles. The most interesting was between Chernyshevsky, Olga Sokratovna, and all of Saratov."

Belotsvetov very nearly smiled at this, but quickly suppressed the impulse, because Yuliya Golova was speaking with disarming sincerity.

"I wanted to talk to you about yesterday's ghost. For Christ's sake, tell me what it looked like, this ghost?"

"Well to be honest, I couldn't make him out clearly. I was very frightened. I'm coming out of the kitchen, and he's standing . . ."

"A man?"

"Yes, only old, or to be more accurate, an old-timer."

"Where exactly was he standing?"

"In front of the mirror in the entrance hall, but he wasn't looking at himself in the mirror, he was standing with his back to it and looking at me, like a statue."

Yuliya Golova sighed gracefully. At that very second, as she was sighing gracefully, a strange transformation overtook Belotsvetov. Something in the distance had caught his attention, at which his face suddenly expressed dread, indignation, and disgust. For a while he looked to be in that state of inner turmoil an ill-natured buffoon might scoff at with, "the cat likes fish but hates to get wet," but then his eyes darkened with determination.

"Excuse me, Yuliya, I'm going to leave you for a minute," he said in an urgent tone and rushed over to the opposite side of the street.

There, by the liquor store across the street, an unpleasant scene was unfolding: a couple of guys in black quilted jackets and black satin coveralls were taking a string bag full of empty bottles away from an elderly idiot. The fellows likely had nothing to get drunk on and, out of despair, had set their sights on the bottles. The idiot was babbling on about something, grimacing fiercely, and waving his free hand around, but despite such lively resistance, he was obviously on the verge of being deprived of his string bag.

Belotsvetov arrived to rescue the idiot, who was holding onto the string bag with his last two fingers, just in the nick of time, as the saying goes, and the unpleasant scene immediately grew into a street-wide event, that was settled, however, in a matter of seconds. For no reason at all the idiot fell down, and his bottles smashed on the pavement, while the guys in the quilted jackets and coveralls attacked the intercessor, as if he had it coming, as if they'd been waiting just for him, as if beating him up were more important to them even than getting drunk again. With lightning speed, they gave Belotsvetov a good going over and then took to their heels.

Belotsvetov stood by the liquor store for another two or three minutes, absorbing the disapproving glares of passersby, because in Russia, no matter what the circumstances, if there's one person who gets no sympathy it's the one on the receiving end of a beating. Then slowly, as if on his last legs, he returned to the waiting Yuliya Golova.

"Now, where were we?" said Belotsvetov, in a deliberately serious tone. Wincing in pain, he touched his brow.

Yuliya shrugged her shoulders inimically.

"We were at the point," Belotsvetov answered for her, "where the ghost was standing with its back to the mirror and looking at you, like a statue. By the way, did you happen to make out how he was dressed?"

"He was dressed unusually," replied Yuliya Golova slowly, "I remember that clearly."

"What do you mean, unusually? Out of style or something?"

"Well no, it's not so much that it was out of style. Just unusually, that is, old-fashioned. As a matter of fact, I'd say he was in uniform, because I perfectly remember bright metallic buttons and either an order or a medal as well . . ."

"Praise thy wonders, O Lord!" uttered Belotsvetov and fell silent.

They started back in the opposite direction since they'd missed their turn while they were talking.

"And do you know who fits your description?" asked Belotsvetov a little while later. "Ensign Ostroumov, the one who shot himself dead in our apartment . . . !"

Yuliya was so taken aback she broke her stride, but then she thought about it for a moment and said:

"Listen, Nikita, you don't seriously believe in ghosts, do you?"

"Well, I'd be happy not to believe in them but, after all, you did see something of the kind, and in a uniform of the old order at that . . . !"

"Maybe it wasn't a ghost at all, only a stranger who'd gotten into our apartment. Or maybe it wasn't a ghost or a stranger — maybe I was sleepwalking."

"A stranger would hardly have found it necessary to deck himself out in an old uniform before stealing into the apartment. And as for sleepwalking, I think what you saw was too vivid for that."

"What's right is right. I can see him dead on, as if it were now — he's standing there, arrogantly, staring like a statue, and silent."

"Now that's a factor I've completely lost sight of: he didn't say a single word?"

"No," answered Yuliya and sighed. "The moment I saw him the silence was extraordinary, but there was a foul smell instead . . ."

"Things are going from bad to worse! What kind of smell was it exactly, were you able to recognize it?"

"It was like the smell of old eggs when you fry them."

"But of course, we should've expected as much: burnt sulfur."

"Burnt sulfur — what does that mean?"

"Burnt sulfur means an evil spirit. You're either pulling my leg, Yuliya, or ghosts are as bitter a reality as drunken bullies."

"By the way, why did you go butt in and fight with them? Are you lacking in adventure or something?!"

"I've got plenty of adventure," said Belotsvetov and touched his brow again. "What's really lacking, though, is action. What I mean is, for some reason a whole national frontier has been set up in this country between conviction and action . . ."

"Why are you telling me all this?" interrupted Yuliya Golova.

"Because I've decided to sever all intermediate links between word and deed and proceed directly from word to deed. See, the day before yesterday, I decided I would fight tooth and nail against every evil, in whatever form I encountered it — and I'm doing just that . . . !"

By the time these words were spoken, the two were already standing in front of their building. Yuliya grabbed the door handle, looked Belotsvetov coldly in the eyes, and said:

"Now I understand why you're a bachelor."

Having returned to Apartment 12, Belotsvetov popped into his room just for a minute to throw off his coat before heading right for Chinarikov's to report what Yuliya Golova had just told him.

Chinarikov was lying on his divan, reading *The Phenomenology of Mind*. Belotsvetov sauntered from the window over to the door a few times, touching his brow, ruffling his hair, rubbing his hands together. Vasily sat up, put his book aside, and asked:

"Well, and what can we congratulate you on?"

"Today you can congratulate me on getting beaten up over by our liquor store. Two drunken bullies were tormenting some little idiot, I came to his defense, and they took it out on my face — which was to be expected, naturally."

"Show me those creeps tomorrow — I'll tear their heads off!"

"And what next! That's all we need now — a vendetta! You'd be better off listening to what I've managed to find out . . ."

Belotsvetov briefly retold Vasily what he'd found out about the ghost that had appeared to Yuliya Golova on Friday.

"So, it wasn't Vanya the locksmith after all . . ." said Chinarikov with a disappointed look, summing up Belotsvetov's story.

"It sure doesn't look like it."

"As a matter of fact, any fool could've dressed himself up as Ensign Ostroumov to jangle everyone's nerves. Mitka Nachalov, for one, is capable of anything . . ."

"No, I was wrong about the ensign. In my opinion he would have been a young man during the Revolution, and Yuliya saw an old man. Therefore, Vasily, it was someone else who appeared to her . . ."

"No offense, Nikita, but I flat-out reject the ghost scenario. Have you gone mad? What kind of ghosts could there be as the curtain falls on the twentieth century?! On Friday evening Yuliya simply happened upon a guy in the entrance hall who'd gotten into the apartment in order to bump off and drag our old lady away. I submit the following scenario: somebody who wished to have

Pumpianskaya disappear from the face of the earth first made sure by phoning that she was home, then he dressed up in a way that would terrify her and induce a state of nervous shock, then sneaked into the apartment, having unlocked the door with a key, which isn't all that difficult to fit, but here he happened upon Yulka, and he disappeared . . . only to reappear an hour later."

"And the smell of burnt sulfur?" asked Belotsvetov.

"Oh, go on with your sulfur! What are you, a materialist or a village granny?!"

"I'm a materialist, of course. But if life has taught me one thing, it's that everything is possible. I'm afraid in this life there isn't anything that would be theoretically impossible . . ."

"Meaning, you're a village granny and not a materialist," said Chinarikov firmly, and he lit up a smoke. "But that's not important right now. Right now what's important is to somehow unearth a sinister old man; we'll sort out the orientation of your world-view some other time. So, it looks as if the evildoer is a man in his declining years, we might say an old man."

"Or a middle-aged person, disguised as an old man."

"Or a middle-aged person, disguised as an old man . . . Of course not! Now why on earth would someone appear in costume if he's going to commit cold-blooded murder?! It was definitely an old man, and the only old man in our whole apartment, it so happens, is Lev Borisovich Fondervyakin . . . ! The next day he was even behaving strangely. He got plastered first thing in the morning and promised the guys from the ambulance service a body . . ."

"Only I have my doubts about the cold-blooded murder," said Belotsvetov, and he sat down beside Chinarikov on the divan.

"If murder really was committed in Pumpianskaya's room, there should've been signs of a struggle, or at least some disarray. But if you remember, the old lady's room was as tidy as on the eve of the October holidays. Except that there was an empty space gaping on the wall, and there was an open box of Seduxen on the sideboard . . ."

"First of all, the culprit could've stunned her with something initially, or lured her from her room and killed her, say, on the backstairs. Second, he had enough time to clean everything up, to cover his tracks. Third, you didn't mention anything to me about Seduxen before."

"At first I didn't pay any attention to it. I only remembered today that there was an open package of Seduxen on the sideboard."

"It's a detail! It's a detail that indicates Alexandra Sergeyevna was seriously upset. Either the very appearance of the sinister old man upset her, or he informed her of something that upset her."

"You know what I'm wondering?" said Belotsvetov, and he wiped his face with the palm of his hand. "How it is the police manage to track down any criminals at all! We seem to have leads to follow and motives to probe, but who? what? when? — that's shrouded in mystery. And it's no small wonder — eight million Muscovites plus visitors . . ."

"We need to talk to Petka," suggested Chinarikov. "Maybe he noticed something interesting while he was sitting on the chamber pot."

He got up from the divan and went to get Petka. Less than a minute later he led him into the room, sat him in the brocade chair, and thrust his hand into his jeans pocket for a smoke.

"Listen, Pyotr," said Belotsvetov, "when you were sitting in the kitchen on the chamber pot on Friday night, did you happen to notice anything interesting?"

"Who's that, Uncle Vas?" asked Pyotr, pointing his finger at the bust of Apukhtin.

"You can ask questions later," said Chinarikov sternly.

"I didn't notice anything interesting. I was just sitting there, that's all. And I didn't see who was in the bathroom, either."

"Was there really someone in the bathroom at the time?" said Belotsvetov, astounded, and he looked over at Chinarikov, who was so startled he snapped the cigarette he was holding.

"I don't know," answered Pyotr lazily. "Mitka just asked me did I see someone in the bathroom or not."

"When he was 'rationing' your air this is what he was interested in?" asked Chinarikov, squatting down diplomatically.

"No. He wanted me to show him a photograph."

"What photograph?"

"The one I found in the yard yesterday. Only it was torn up. I picked it up and taped it back together."

"Let's see it," demanded Chinarikov, his voice shaking with impatience.

Pyotr was unsure if he should comply with Chinarikov's demand so readily, even sticking his index finger into his mouth, but here Belotsvetov interjected:

"I give you permission to set my door on fire, feed my new boots to the dogs, paint all over my jacket with watercolors, but for the love of God just show us the photograph . . ."

Blushing, apparently in earnest at such an entertaining prospect, Pyotr yielded. He took off his left slipper and pulled out a photograph, folded in four.

It was of a solemn-looking old man in a civilian service uniform, on which could be seen a cross, seemingly of the Order of St. Stanislaus.

"Well, what's the verdict?" Chinarikov said.

"To begin with," responded Belotsvetov, "the verdict is that it's the same photograph that was hanging in Pumpianskaya's room and later vanished into thin air under mysterious circumstances."

"Alexandra Sergeyevna could've taken it with her," added Chinarikov, "when she abandoned our apartment for good on Friday night. A sinister old man arrived, ordered her to get ready, and right then and there she took the photograph. By the way, this assumes that Alexandra Sergeyevna knew she was indeed abandoning the apartment for good."

"Alright, but then why did she tear up the photograph?"

"Yes, that makes no sense of course . . . Then I guess it was the sinister old man who decided to destroy the photograph, because it could tip somebody off."

"What I find interesting," said Belotsvetov, somewhat fervently, "is that this old man in uniform is likely who appeared to Yuliya Golova on Friday as well. Hold on a minute, I'll be right back . . ."

Belotsvetov left Chinarikov's room, having hidden the photograph in the breast pocket of his shirt.

"Uncle Vas, tell me something about the war," Pyotr asked.

"Nah . . ."

"Come on, tell me — what does it cost you . . . !"

"The hell with that! It's better if I sing you a war song . . ."

Pyotr nodded merrily in consent, while Chinarikov grew glum, propped his head up with his fist, and began to sing:

"Only an echo will resound through the hills / And my soul will fly home / In his land Allah is behind every rock / But who will protect me, an orphan . . ."

"Just as I suspected!" said Belotsvetov upon his return. "This is the same old man Yuliya saw on Friday. She even turned pale, poor thing, when I showed her the photograph . . ."

"That's excellent!" exclaimed Chinarikov. "This means we've established who the culprit is. Now we only have to find him and nab him!"

"That's interesting. How are you going to nab him when he's been in the grave for at least forty years . . . !"

"He hasn't turned up from beyond the grave?!"

"That's just it . . ."

Chinarikov fell obliviously silent, and on his face appeared that pained, sheepish look seen on children who've stumbled upon certain secrets of adult existence.

"And what makes you think this old man is, in fact, deceased?" he objected timidly.

"Let's do the math," proposed Belotsvetov. "The photograph was taken no later than 1918, because by 1919 they weren't wearing uniforms like these, and certainly not with the Order of St. Stanislaus. By that time the old man would've been a minimum of fifty, although he looks a lot older. That would make him 118 today."

"And? Surely it's not impossible to live to the age of 118?"

"Of course it's possible, but at that age a person wouldn't go out on a wet job."

"We'll just have to wait and see."

"Listen Vasily, this conversation is turning silly!"

Chinarikov's expression clouded over, but by all indications he agreed with that assessment.

"Nonetheless," he said, "it would be well to inquire about any old men who've turned 120 — after all, this is the sort of thread you were looking for."

"Shouldn't we at least show the photograph to Kuznetsova and Sarantsev in case they know this old man . . . ?"

Chinarikov was on the point of responding to Belotsvetov's suggestion, when the door to the room opened slightly, and Mitya's head pushed through the crack.

"What do you want?" said Chinarikov irritably.

"I've got an extraordinary announcement to make," said Mitya, and he squinted his eyes unsympathetically at Pyotr. "Only I can't say what in the presence of minors."

Chinarikov unceremoniously sent Pyotr packing and impatiently uttered: "Well?"

"I've just discovered a letter addressed to Pumpianskaya in our mailbox." And Mitya held out an envelope to Chinarikov.

The envelope was ordinary enough, with a four-kopek stamp, a portrait of Academician Vernadsky, and the address on it was written in the violet ink of the post office.

Chinarikov flipped the envelope over and looked at Belotsvetov with eyes that seemed to say that although it didn't suit a well-bred person to read someone else's mail, it couldn't be helped, the envelope had to be torn open, to which Belotsvetov shrugged his shoulders as if to say no argument here, that ethics are a fine thing but given the existing circumstances, naturally this was not the time for them. That's when Chinarikov tore open the envelope.

In it was a narrow strip of checked paper that had been cut out of an exercise book. Fairly large letters were pasted onto it, composing the following message: "You will return the documents on Wednesday. Or else — death."

Chinarikov passed the note to Belotsvetov and asked:

"Well, what's the verdict?"

Belotsvetov passed the note to Mitya Nachalov and replied:

"In light of such sudden twists, I've lost the ability to reach any verdict whatsoever."

"What do you say, Dmitry?"

"I think there's something fishy about it," said Mitya pensively. "Just the same, our old lady was probably mixed up in some sort of intrigue. Or she wasn't mixed up in anything, but was safeguarding documents exposing a crime."

"And I think," said Chinarikov, "the first thing we ought to do is investigate the letter thoroughly. Take the envelope: the outgoing postmark is smudged, but it seems the letter was likely sent last Tuesday and it arrived at our district post office today — that postmark is clear. The last point about the envelope: since the address is written with an ordinary dip pen in violet ink, it was addressed at the post office."

"Does the handwriting tell you anything?" asked Belotsvetov absent-mindedly.

"Oddly enough, the handwriting is most likely a woman's. What's interesting about the note, in my opinion, is that the letters have been cut out of a children's book. They're oversized, and the print is overly saturated."

"And what does this tell you?"

"Only that the letters were cut out of a children's book."

The room fell silent. Mitya fingered the note, Belotsvetov's unseeing eyes scrutinized the teacups bearing portraits of

Napoleon's marshals, Chinarikov turned things over in his mind.

"And do you know who killed Alexandra Sergeyevna?" announced Chinarikov after about a minute.

"Who?" exhaled Belotsvetov in a fright, while Mitya Nachalov showed he was on the alert with his eyes and a particular tilt of the head.

"The post office! More precisely, a postal district! You see, in sending the letter by post on Tuesday, the murderer reasonably supposed that Alexandra Sergeyevna would receive it on Wednesday morning, because he might even have been sending it from a nearby street. Had Alexandra Sergeyevna actually received the letter on Wednesday morning, she probably would've handed the secret documents over to the murderer from fright, but because of our disgraceful postal service the letter arrived not on Wednesday, but on Sunday, as though it hadn't been posted from Moscow to Moscow, but from Los Angeles to Moscow. Meaning, the post office is the real culprit — or at least an accomplice to the heinous crime . . . !"

"This is no time for jokes, Vasily!" Belotsvetov interrupted him. "No, it surely is not! Because with this letter the matter has become too serious. Such criminal depths and perspectives are coming to light here, it's time Rybkin got involved."

"Not on your life!" said Chinarikov heatedly. "We started this business and we'll finish it. Otherwise, it's 'thanks very much, boys, now step aside.' We've all but established who the culprit is, worked through a few scenarios, questioned a hundred people — and make a gift of all this to Rybkin?! No, suit yourself, but I'm not about to build his career with my own hands . . ."

"What on earth are you blathering on about? When exactly did we establish who the culprit is?"

"Hello, but didn't you and I just come to the conclusion that the culprit is a 118-year-old geezer who had some sort of long-term relationship with Alexandra Sergeyevna . . . ?"

Belotsvetov didn't respond to that. He just looked at Chinarikov condescendingly, as they say.

"Didn't you and I just work out the optimal crime scenario?" continued Chinarikov. "A 118-year-old geezer, on whom our Alexandra Sergeyevna had some compromising material, writes her a letter on Tuesday demanding the return of the material and threatening her with pain of death. Due to the silent sabotage at the post office, he doesn't receive a reply, so on Friday night he first finds out by phoning if his victim is at home, and then he turns up in our apartment and stumbles upon Yuliya Golova. Sometime later he comes back and so frightens Alexandra Sergeyevna she's forced to take Seduxen, after which he takes back the documents, removes a photograph of himself from the wall to cover his tracks, leads the unfortunate old woman out to the street, kills her, and hides the corpse."

"And why not?" said Mitya Nachalov. "It really looks like that's exactly how it happened."

"For it to have happened exactly like that," said Belotsvetov perceptively, "there would have to be at least one 118-year-old man living in Moscow."

"Why the geographic restrictions?" asked Chinarikov, forcing a smile. "He could be in Moscow province, Syzran, or even in Kzyl-Orda."

"Alright, but why is the address on the envelope written in a woman's hand?"

"Good Lord! So he asked the first old lady he came across at the post office, and she wrote out the address . . . !"

"Alright, but why did the culprit smudge the outgoing postmark?"

"To conceal his own locality."

"Alright, why on earth did he go out on a wet job dressed up in a uniform, with a cross on it no less — why such an elaborate masquerade?"

Chinarikov parted his hands lugubriously.

At this point there was a knock on the door, and in walked Valenchik.

"I would ask you all to the kitchen," he said solemnly.

It was now around seven o'clock in the evening.

4

While Chinarikov and Belotsvetov were selflessly unraveling the mystery behind Alexandra Sergeyevna Pumpianskaya's disappearance, in Apartment 12 it was business as usual, as the saying goes. Fondervyakin played chess with Dushkin for several hours straight. At first they bickered, since Dushkin had announced his pretensions to the vacated room to Fondervyakin as well, but one word led to another and their arguing soon turned to pawns aspiring to be queens, and it quickly became clear that both men shared a passion for chess. Anna Olegovna Kapitonova lay down for a nap after lunch. Before showing up at Chinarikov's with the letter from the murderer, Mitya Nachalov had gone out for a walk, and then read a few pages of *War and Peace* when he returned — in particular, the scene where Pierre Bezukhov meets Karataev. Yuliya Golova, having fed her brood, got down to an issue of *Burda*, and at the very moment when Belotsvetov showed up at her place with the photograph of the ghost, she was copying examples of eveningwear into a special notebook. Lyubov, meanwhile, was doing her homework for Monday. At first, Pyotr loafed around the corridor, then he went for a walk, and then he loafed around the corridor again. Genrikh Valenchik was writing something, while Vera Valenchik just sat there like a sack of potatoes.

Between six and seven that evening Fondervyakin and Dushkin, both a bit slaphappy from their match, tumbled out into the corridor.

"Listen, Lyova," said Dushkin thoughtfully, "do you know why I'm here?"

"What's that?" asked Fondervyakin, prompting him to repeat the question.

"Can you say why I've dropped by your apartment?"

"Looks as if you wanted to get a good look at the vacant room. Not on your life, though. That room's not for you to see any more than your ears are."

"Ech, Lyova, Lyova, you don't know me very well! I'm a simple man, you might even say blunt. If I decide on something, I'll get my way come hell or high water."

Anna Olegovna came into the corridor from her room in a chintz dressing gown, her head a tangle of violet ringlets and, stumbling upon Dushkin with her glance, stared at him wide-eyed in sleepy astonishment.

"Feast your eyes on this, Anna Olegovna," said Fondervyakin, presenting the locksmith to her with a certain flourish of his arms. "Yet another pretender to the vacant room!"

"It's disgusting," said Anna Olegovna, without any particular show of disgust. "Over my dead body! An outsider will move into our apartment only over my dead body! You've already done one old lady in, Comrades, and you'll have to do in another . . ."

"Oh for goodness' sake," implored Fondervyakin cloyingly, "you're hardly an old lady, now, are you?"

The remark provoked a stern response from Kapitonova:

"Thank you for the compliment, of course," she said, "but I won't give up that room for anything in the world!"

"You talk about it as if it were yours already," remarked Fondervyakin sullenly.

"It will be mine — it's not going anywhere!"

"And on what grounds is it to be yours?"

"If nothing else, because Pumpianskaya's room is adjacent to ours. Just hack a door through and it's an apartment within an apartment . . ."

"Don't argue, people," interrupted Dushkin. "No need to waste your words and nerves on nothing, because I'm the one moving into that room no matter what."

"Over my dead body!" confirmed Anna Olegovna.

Hearing the commotion, Valenchik leaned out into the corridor.

"Has something else happened?" he asked in a fright.

"There has," answered Fondervyakin and turned away. "They've all swooped in like hawks for the vacant room!"

"And to hell with me, right?"

"You said it."

"In that case, I see only one way out of the situation: everyone needs to assemble, like we did in '80, and decide the housing question on democratic grounds. Let the people decide who is to stay where they are and who gets to live high on the hog in two rooms.

It's high time we assimilated democracy, Comrades — after all, the seventieth anniversary of Soviet power is upon us!"

"But, the people — that's us," objected Fondervyakin. "So each of us will decide in favor of himself living high on the hog in two rooms."

"We'll be clever about it . . . We'll select a committee and give it a mandate to consider the question in all its complexity and then to take the appropriate decision."

"We ought to invite someone from the housing office," proposed Fondervyakin, "or else we'll have our democracy and they'll have theirs."

"I've got nothing against it. Lev Borisovich, you go ahead and call Vostryakova, and I'll notify our fellow tenants."

"Go ahead, notify them," agreed Dushkin snidely. "You've got your democracy, the housing office has got theirs, but I'll do things in my own downhome way, people, and you'll see, as the saying goes: 'Might makes right.' "

"What do you mean?" asked Valenchik sternly.

"That's a secret for now."

About ten minutes later the entire population of Apartment 12 was gathered in the kitchen, with the exception of Belotsvetov, who was slightly delayed, and including the locksmith Dushkin, who was cheerfully leaning on his elbow against the stove. Vera Valenchik came with her own chair; Genrikh had even put on a clean shirt, a bold brown check, and combed his hair for the occasion; Fondervyakin stood by the kitchen table and tapped nervously on the windowpane with his fingernails; Anna Olegovna was nervous as well, now examining the midriff section of her dress, now adjusting her violet ringlets; Mitya Nachalov was quietly brooding;

Chinarikov, having shown up in his eternal jeans and short-sleeved T-shirt, which hid his airborne forces tattoo, occupied the position by the door to the backstairs; Yuliya Golova leafed through her fashion magazine; Lyubov came with her Latin textbook; Pyotr sat on the stool, dangling his legs.

"Comrades and Neighbors!" Genrikh Valenchik was just beginning when a prolonged ringing sounded in the entrance hall, and he had to break off.

There was the sound of the door opening, then footsteps, and then Vostryakova, the building superintendent, appeared in the kitchen in a snow-white nylon jacket and started to bawl out:

"Have you no conscience, Citizens?! You won't let a person rest even on a Sunday . . . !"

"We'll rest in the grave," said Fondervyakin gloomily, and for some reason this observation pacified Vostryakova.

The last to appear was Belotsvetov, who looked anxious and somber, pained even.

"Well, alright," asked Vostryakova conciliatorily, "what's the matter here?"

"You're about to find out everything," Valenchik told her, and since his subsequent words were addressed to the whole gathering, he abruptly transformed himself: he straightened up, assumed a grave expression, placed his hand on his hip, and even seemed to become somewhat thinner in the face. "Comrade Neighbors!" he began, "we have gathered here in order to elect a committee of tenants. The days of obscurantism are over — I say this in all earnestness. The times are such that democracy and glasnost decide everything. So let's go ahead and elect a committee democratically, say of three persons, and let them decide, under conditions of glasnost, who moves into the freed-up living space. We'll begin by nominating the candidature . . ."

But nobody was preparing to nominate the candidature. Everyone was silent. Everyone was so profoundly silent that the water could be heard dripping from the faucet. Finally, Anna Olegovna declared:

"It's easy to say 'nominate the candidature'! But who to nominate — that's the problem! No matter who we propose, each of us has an interest in Pumpianskaya's little room."

Again, silence.

"Well, what's keeping you, Comrades?" implored Valenchik. "Shake a leg! Shake a leg!"

"I nominate myself," said Fondervyakin, knitting his brows since he was anticipating energetic objection.

"Oh no you don't, not on your life!," exclaimed Yuliya Golova. "Every idiot knows you're aiming to grab Pumpianskaya's room to use as a pantry . . . !"

"This is an altogether un-Soviet formulation of the question," remarked Valenchik, and Vera agreed with him on spousal grounds, with a certain devoted movement of her head. "Self-interest of this kind reeks of bourgeois parliamentarianism from a mile away . . ."

And Genrikh Valenchik began conscientiously to explain why Fondervyakin's suggestion reeked of bourgeois parliamentarianism.

"What held you up?" Chinarikov whispered to Belotsvetov, who'd been staring at the floor the whole time.

"Well, you see, it suddenly occurred to me to leaf through Petka's books . . ." Belotsvetov said.

"You leafed through them?"

"I did . . . Thirty-three letters, two periods, and one dash have been cut out of the children's book *Silver Hoof*. Consequently, however absurd it might seem, the letter with the death threat originated in Yuliya Golova's family . . ."

Chinarikov raised his eyebrows, but a large enameled pot standing on the windowsill caught his eye, and his mouth watered involuntarily as the strong, cool smell of borscht reached his nostrils.

"Listen here, Professor, you know, we haven't even had breakfast this morning on account of these forensics!"

Belotsvetov nodded absent-mindedly and was once again lost in contemplation of the floor.

". . . and we do not wish to pander to these foreign tendencies," said Valenchik, who in the meantime was finishing up his speech. "So then, Lev Borisovich, let's have the withdrawal of your self-nomination!"

"Withdrawal," repeated Pyotr loudly, who'd obviously simply taken a liking to the word.

"No, Comrades," said Kapitonova, "we'll never get anywhere this way. This democracy business is hokum, because Lev Borisovich wants to snap up the room as his pantry, Yuliya's got two kids, one of each sex, Genrikh could use a study, and to be honest, I've got Dmitry. So what kind of democracy can there be here?! Let's not waste anymore time and decide this matter by the age-old folk method — casting lots."

"Well, of course!" said Lyuba. "We'll cast lots, and Nikita Ivanovich will end up with the room even though he could give a fig about it!"

"Or let's handle it this way," proposed Fondervyakin. "Let's cut out the shenanigans, Comrades, and all agree that the living space should go to me. I'm almost an old man, dammit all, and I've gone through fire, water, and the fight against cosmopolitanism — so have I really not earned a pantry from my Motherland?!"

Genrikh Valenchik took no notice of this proposition.

"So then," he said, "are there any ideas for the candidature?"

Surprising everyone, Genrikh's Vera took the floor:

"I propose we select a committee of persons," she said, "who have no interest in augmenting their living space. In other words, I nominate Vasily and Nikita as candidates."

"And the third?" asked Genrikh.

"Let the third candidate be Vera," suggested Fondervyakin. "Even though she's expecting a new arrival in the family, in my opinion she doesn't give a hoot about augmenting her living space."

"Right you are," said Vera dolefully.

"Only, the candidates have got to carefully consider our critical situation," beseeched Yuliya Golova.

"It goes without saying," replied Fondervyakin.

"So then, are there any further nominations?" asked Genrikh Valenchik, and after a very short pause he answered his own question: "No further nominations. Then we'll proceed to the secret vote. Here's a matchbox . . ."

Vostryakova interrupted him:

"Just a moment, Citizens, are you serious?"

"What do you mean by 'serious,' " asked Valenchik.

"Do you seriously intend to assign living space in this way?"

Save for Dushkin, everyone answered affirmatively.

"In that case, Citizens, I officially declare that there will be no casting of lots! However the housing office decides the fate of this little room is what we'll all abide by!

"Oh no you don't, Comrade Vostryakova!" said Fondervyakin.

"After all, it's not '37, and we're not going to tolerate any bureaucratic dictates."

"Right, only come now, Comrades, we can do without this . . . without personal attacks and threats. Especially since our communal tenants would not flout democracy and glasnost. Surely they would not be so brazen as to commit such an utterly hostile act as to oppose the elemental force of the people . . ."

Vostryakova grew so thoughtful her face darkened.

"So then," continued Valenchik, "let's proceed to the secret vote . . . Here's a matchbox with exactly seven matches in it, corresponding to the number of eligible voters: whoever votes in favor of the nominated candidates returns the match to the box in its original state; whoever votes against Nikita breaks off the head of the match; whoever votes against Vaska puts half a match back into the box; whoever votes against Vera leaves behind a tiny stub."

"What an incomprehensible electoral system," said Anna Olegovna, looking around dully at the gathering. "And supposing I want to cast a vote against Vera but for Nikita?"

"Then you leave the head on the match and gnaw off a tiny stub from the opposite end."

"And for Vera and Nikita but against Vasily?"

"Then just break the match into two pieces of equal length."

"No," pronounced Fondervyakin crossly, "I don't agree to such capricious voting rules! We'll become confused as hell, or for all we know there'll be all kinds of fraud . . ."

"Oh, to hell with these elections . . . ," proposed Chinarikov. "Why don't we make a memorial out of Alexandra Sergeyevna's room and not offend anyone or worry our heads over these foolish elections . . ."

"I'm interested in something else," interjected Lyubov. "How is it that all of you can vote and Dmitry and I can't? Is that what you call democracy?"

"Shush!" her mother cut her off.

Fondervyakin put his arms akimbo, looked at Chinarikov cruelly, and said:

"As for myself, Vasily, I reject your outrageous proposal outright! Just imagine dreaming up such a thing: Vera's due any second now, Yuliya's huddled up with two kids, a deserving person's got nowhere to stick sixteen jars . . ."

"Fifteen now," corrected Mitya.

". . . fifteen jars of preserved apples, and this character's proposing to give away a perfectly habitable lodging to serve as some memorial!"

"Not just any memorial," clarified Vasily, "but a memorial to communal living, to the humble Soviet person's way of life in general. You cranks! In another fifteen years the rising generation won't have any understanding of how fathers and sons suffered privation and hardship! Look at Dmitry and Lyubov — they're the last generation of Soviet people who'll remember the harsh legacy of War Communism . . . !"

"I only wish I could forget," Yuliya Golova put in.

"I wouldn't go that far," objected Valenchik. "Suit yourselves, Comrades, but all the same, communal apartments were universities of newly structured human relations. Bitter universities to be sure, but they've left us more than kitchen brawls and kerosene-tainted cabbage soups, they've also left us . . . I'd even call it an attachment to family life, which for the time being still glimmers in our people. Wouldn't you say so . . . ?"

"Yes," said Fondervyakin, "all sorts of things went on — both good and bad. Only when I think back on having survived the Sizov gang and Plenipotentiary Kulakov, for instance, it sends shivers down my spine!"

"But let's not forget," Anna Olegovna stepped in, "what friendly terms we were on during the Olympics! What I mean to say is that in our blessed Apartment 12 we've not only had bad come with the good, we've also had good come with the bad. Here's a concrete example for you: Petka and Lyubov are someone else's kids, but they seem like our own. By the way, Lyubov, you'd better open the door to the backstairs, you can hardly breathe in here . . ."

Annoyed, Lyubov got up from her seat and opened the backdoor, through which a draft of cool, damp air was felt at once.

"I suppose on the whole," said Belotsvetov, "the system of communal living has played such a great role in the development of our national character that historians will have their hands full investigating this phenomenon for years and years to come. All kidding aside, somehow our family-oriented lifestyle is, as they say, a fact, and even if communal living is only partly responsible, then we ought to say 'thank you very much,' in spite of the kerosene-tainted cabbage soups, brawls, and other disgraceful goings-on."

"Well in my opinion this is all just crude socialism," said Yuliya Golova. "And I must admit, I don't understand why you're all so moved . . ."

"As for me," answered Fondervyakin, "I'm moved by the fact that in a communal apartment everything is in the presence of others, out in the open. You sure wouldn't drive your daughter-in-law to suicide here. Generally speaking, you don't allow yourself to behave just any old way, but more or less in the interest of the collective. Come to think of it, on account of this our destinies are carbon copies, too, so to speak. Now then, Pyotr, how does that Vysotsky song about Kiska go?"

Pyotr smoothed down a light brown tuft of hair that had popped up on the back of his head and with the fixed expression of a balladeer sang out: *You too have been victimized / As you've been Russified / Mine are missing in action / Yours sit innocent in jail . . .*

At the last line, the doorbell rang in the entrance hall, and Mitya Nachalov rushed over to open the door. He returned accompanied by a strange couple, whose appearance astonished everyone, with the exception of Belotsvetov, because they were Sarantsev and Kuznetsova.

"These, Comrades, are relatives of our Pumpianskaya," Belotsvetov explained to the gathering.

"And to what, as the saying goes, do we owe their visit?" asked Valenchik striking an official tone.

"What do you mean 'to what'?" repeated Kuznetsova, with slight indignation. "We're not just anybody, we're your neighbor's kinfolk, and she's left some belongings behind, and I reckon you could register someone in her room retroactively . . ."

"Twelve men on a dead man's chest!" interjected Mitya and smiled sarcastically.

"Let's assume the old woman's belongings are negligible," declared Valenchik, "I say this in earnest . . ."

"Come now," Kuznetsova stopped him. "Her Japanese sapling alone is worth as much as a Zhiguli."

"As far as the room goes," said Yuliya Golova, " there are enough pretenders to it without you."

"Jesus Christ!" exclaimed Kapitonova. "What the heck is going on here — half of Moscow has congregated for ten square meters . . . !"

"Don't worry, Anna Olegovna," Fondervyakin reassured her, "we won't give that little room away to any outsiders, and they won't get her pitiable belongings except through the courts."

"What's with all these bureaucratic obstacles?" asked Alyosha Sarantsev. "Surely we can decide the matter on humanitarian grounds . . ."

"Really, Comrades," said Chinarikov to support him, and he smiled soothingly. "They're not just anybody, but kinfolk . . ."

"The devil only knows what kind of kinfolk they are!" Anna Olegovna said.

"And what remarkable cheek!" added Yuliya Golova. "Imagine dreaming up such an idea: registering someone retroactively in a perfect stranger's room!"

"Incidentally, people," reminded Dushkin, "do you think you might still get around to assigning the vacant room?"

"What do you think we're doing here?" said Genrikh Valenchik, and he jabbed Dushkin in the ribs with his elbow. "We're proceeding in all sincerity. It's just that all kinds of ignorant relatives are showing up and preventing us from doing our business. So then: here's the matchbox . . ."

"Just a moment, Genrikh," his wife stopped him. "Shouldn't we first decide if we even want to acknowledge the pretensions of Alexandra Sergeyevna's relatives to the freed-up room?"

Alyosha Sarantsev forestalled the all too obvious reaction to this question:

"Personally, I don't need the room," he said, putting his right hand to his chest. "But as to my aunt's belongings, I would ask that you place them at our disposal without any bureaucratic foot-dragging."

"That does it! My patience is exhausted!" said Dushkin, interrupting the argument. "If you're too busy to sort things out with the vacant room, people, then I'll resolve this particular housing issue as I see fit." Whereupon he turned to Vostryakova, sustained a malevolent pause, and continued: "Comrade Vostryakova, it's up to you to assign that little room to me! I demand it not because I need it, but on principle, to stick it to this intelligentsia! Or else I quit!"

Evidently, this was a well-founded threat since Vostryakova's face immediately took on a submissive, defenseless expression.

"What a bastard!" hissed Yuliya Golova.

"And that, Comrades, is my surprise. Even if you file a complaint at the UN against our housing office, I'll still be the one moving into the little old lady's room!"

"For crying out loud, Comrades?!" Fondervyakin started to say with wounded alarm. "Why, this is banditry of the blackest dye!"

"Do you hold yourself accountable for your words?" asked Dushkin insinuatingly.

"I certainly do hold myself fully accountable for my words. You are a petty swindler with subversive tendencies! It would seem, Comrades, that his b4 pawn has jumped all the way to b6! You're a cheater, and that's all there is to it!"

"What if I give you one on the dome for that 'cheater' comment?"

"Wha-at?" bawled Fondervyakin, and his bald spot turned terribly red. "You dare threaten me, too? Why you contra, I'll crack your head open with this roaster!"

And Fondervyakin did indeed grab Kapitonova's roaster off the table.

After this dangerous gesture, there immediately followed what in dramaturgy is called a silent scene: District Inspector Rybkin unexpectedly came in through the unlocked backdoor, and at once the kitchen turned to stone. Fondervyakin was left standing just as he was, with the roaster in his right hand; Dushkin's face was frozen in a bellicose snarl; Chinarikov stood motionless in a conciliatory pose, as he had been poised to separate Fondervyakin and Dushkin; and even Pyotr, who was still too young to fear the police, even slightly, held one leg cautiously under his stool and stuck the other one cautiously out in front in a kind of petit battement.

Rybkin walked over to the middle of the kitchen, touched his cap, which had been displaced, as usual, onto the back of his head, looked around impassively at those present, and said:

"I've come to you with sad news, Comrades. This morning the body of your old lady was discovered on a bench at the very top of Pokrovsky Boulevard — and sitting up, poor thing, is how she died."

"Did she die on her own, or was she murdered?" asked Belotsvetov in a voice not his own.

"Definitely on her own. An examination by experts has revealed acute heart failure as a result of hypothermia."

"You mean she'd just been sitting on the bench like that for forty-eight hours?" Chinarikov said.

"Death occurred overnight between Friday and Saturday. Therefore, the old lady had been sitting upright on the bench in a post-mortem state for about thirty hours. Are there any other questions?"

"There aren't any questions," responded Fondervyakin, "only one bitter comment: for crying out loud, what are we coming to?! A dead old woman sitting upright on a bench for thirty hours straight in the very heart of Moscow — and it's as if it were perfectly normal! I mean, in thirty hours not a single skunk walked up and took an interest in her, asked what the heck an old woman like her was doing there, sitting around like that . . ."

Rybkin looked at Fondervyakin sternly and said:

"Since there aren't any questions, come along, Comrades, let's break it up."

And they all started to disperse.

Belotsvetov joined Kuznetsova, and after making one or two polite but idle comments he showed her the photograph he'd earlier cajoled from Pyotr.

"You don't happen to know this person, do you?" he asked, pretending leisurely indifference.

Kuznetsova looked dolefully at the photograph and said:

"How could I not know? It's poor Sasha's father! Sergei Vladimirovich Pumpiansky, collegiate counselor and gentleman, himself."

MONDAY

1

Particularly interesting is this: given the nature of the events that have unfolded in Apartment 12 of the big corner building on Petroverigsky Lane, it's evident that the present narrative is simpler and watered down compared to Dostoevsky's St. Petersburg variant. The people seem to be one and the same, Great Russian. The circumstances are similar, and the plots have a lot in common — after all, both cases show to some extent the woes of wit, a drama that smells of the lamp. But, well, who would have thought it possible: the intensity of life in each is entirely different! Gone are those anguished dispositions and wild outbursts of emotion. Gone are the scrupulousness of being and the painful profundity of thought, from which awe-inspiring scandals are born. Everything now is somehow feeble, half-hearted, ordinary, and, more importantly, character has grown shallow. Even if we assume that Lev Borisovich is a troublemaker and a bit of a juicer, as the saying goes, he's still no Marmeladov. True, District Inspector Rybkin is an arm of the law and hasn't been cheated out of his fair share of a capacity for inductive reasoning, but he's a far cry from Porfiry Petrovich, and not only is Lyubov Golova not Sonya, in this narrative she's quite unremarkable, and to such a degree she's almost completely immaterial — as though she didn't even exist.

Much depends on the penetration of one's gaze and how impressionable one is, of course. Yet the point here is that not only do the innate abilities of the respective narrators differ profoundly, but that the St. Petersburg variant of the drama was rendered in absolute accord with the laws of art, while the present narrative is an attempt to reproduce life in accord with the laws of life itself, of one still being lived, and to establish, if possible, why it is that in paintings the color red is most often rendered as red, while literature makes it a grayish-brown-crimson, and yet it comes out just right, as the common folk say in their charming simplicity. Since attempts of this sort are burdened by the notion that a life put into words is partly literature anyway, only baseless, then what you get is something nondescript, neither fish nor fowl — something bloodless, so to speak, desolate. And it's no wonder, because art is the rule, and life just isolated instances, which only an artist is capable of forming into a meaningful unity charged with a higher purpose. No such notion of higher purpose underlies the isolated instance. Thus, the essence of artistic talent lies in the obscure ability to transform the particular into a whole, one that might be capable of bursting forth into some great truth, or even of creating such a truth out of material that has been utterly depleted of its spirit, not unlike the fired clay bricks used to build beautiful cities.

On the other hand, it's not at all inconceivable that our day and age have witnessed a notable democratization of thought, suffering, and behavior. This could have occurred as a result of more favorable living conditions, with which the spirit finds itself in an inverse relationship, or universally higher levels of education, or because man has simply grown shallow. That's why our life possesses a completely different degree of intensity, and notions of

Napoleonic selfhood no longer occur to anyone, and a bureaucrat just might drink himself down to the status of a porter, but in no way to that of a suicide, and someone who never completed his university degree wouldn't go after an old lady with axe in hand, and nobody would set out "for America" by dint of a lady's revolver, simply out of boredom.

All the more strange is that classical history, broadly speaking, has repeated itself in our dispassionate times in the way that destinies, historical events, or catastrophes sometimes repeat, broadly, as if this history displayed a certain existential invariance, even repeating itself to such extent that on Monday morning, as though out of a clear blue sky, a Luzhin showed up — and not just any Luzhin, but a Pyotr Petrovich Luzhin, who turned out to be an old acquaintance of Yuliya Golova from the city of Yaroslavl, where she had done her training at a chemical plant a very long time ago. In accordance with the laws of literature, Luzhin's appearance would require some sort of dramatic charge, something would have to ensue; but in this case he just showed up, and that was that.

This is the way it happened: around eight o'clock in the morning, when Genrikh and Vera had already left for work, Anna Olegovna was preparing Mitya's breakfast, Yuliya Golova was putting on her face, Chinarikov was getting ready to go hack the ice by building No. 8, Belotsvetov, having awoken at the crack of dawn, was lying on the sofa contemplating the ceiling, the youth were still sleeping, and Fondervyakin was lounging around the kitchen at loose ends, the doorbell rang with a cheerful uneasiness, and a minute later Pyotr Petrovich Luzhin appeared in the entrance hall, declaring right off that he'd be staying at Yuliya Golova's for a couple of days. He turned out to be a noisy, common person, and frank to the point of indecency. For example, not more than fifteen minutes after showing up he was already in the kitchen, recounting how he'd only just divorced his wife purely for physiological reasons, that he'd come to Moscow to find a bride, that he'd taken quite a shine to Lyubov Golova, and that having waited for his beloved to come of age, he would now woo her without fail.

"Well, we'll just see about that," said Mitya in disapproval.

By about nine o'clock in the morning the apartment had quieted down, the studying and toiling contingent of the residents having dispersed each in pursuit of his or her own affairs. Pyotr had gone out for a stroll; Luzhin had lain down for a snooze; Anna Olegovna had gotten down to her *Tales of the Don*, which she'd been chewing over for nearly three months; and Chinarikov and Belotsvetov were just then approaching building No. 8. Since there was a lot they needed to finish discussing, and since Belotsvetov's so-called "library-study day" fell on Mondays, he'd volunteered to help Chinarikov clear the sidewalk in front of building No. 8.

Arriving in concentrated silence, not counting a couple of worthless remarks, Chinarikov armed himself with a crowbar that had an axe blade welded onto its end, and Belotsvetov with an aluminum shovel. No sooner had they gotten down to work than their long-awaited conversation began.

"So what do you think about all this?" asked Belotsvetov, trying out the shovel.

"The same as I did the day before yesterday," answered Chinarikov, exhaling forcefully on the word "yesterday." "There was an old lady, and now she's all gone."

Belotsvetov said mournfully:

"I envy you, Vasily, you're cold-blooded."

"I'm not cold-blooded, I'm mentally adaptable. Follow my example: when I feel like crying I'm a Stoic, and a Zen Buddhist when I want to be. All told, that Asian know-it-all was so right when he said, 'Sit patiently on your own doorstep, and you'll see your enemy carried past you.' "

"That's what I'm saying, you're cold-blooded."

For a few minutes they worked in silence, Chinarikov breaking off chunks of dirty ice with his weird implement and Belotsvetov throwing them onto the road with the shovel. Then Belotsvetov resumed the conversation:

"Here's what I think: some incredible, Mephistophelian sort of story has emerged, one that is out of sync with our times and ways. Such stories were conceivable in the age of the Barbarian Invasions, or in the Bulgakovian twenties, but they're not possible today, they're as out of place as the Wars of the Roses. In the meantime, we're confronted with the following scenario: on Friday evening, in the very center of Moscow, the ghost of Collegiate Counselor Pumpiansky appears and leads his own daughter out onto Pokrovsky Boulevard where she dies of hypothermia; before that, a torn-up photo of the long-deceased old man pops up, Fondervyakin promises the boys from the ambulance service a corpse, and the telephone ringing — possibly from the other world — fills the apartment. That, Vasily, is the sort of scenario we have unfolding."

Catching his breath, Chinarikov said:

"With such a romantic outlook it's a wonder pharmacologists get library-study days at all."

Belotsvetov shivered, not because of Chinarikov's words, but because a few drops of slushy water had dripped down his collar.

The weather had turned out to be disturbingly nasty on this Monday. It was overcast, chilly, even downright cold, yet a distinct trace of spring was in the air, and the roofs dripped accordingly, as if it had begun to drizzle.

"You see, Nikita, here's the thing," continued Chinarikov, still armed with his hybrid crowbar-axe, "even though you're older than me, you're younger all the same. Here's what I mean: what I've seen in my life you couldn't dream up even in your worst nightmares, and that's why I haven't got two kopeks worth of romantic notions left in me. See, you and I think man is the indisputable and supreme value — that's what they taught us anyway. But I've seen with my own eyes this supreme value with its head cut off and rib cage exposed, giving you a clear view of its dried-out heart, which looks more like an old lady's change purse. It's a wonder I haven't been able to swat a fly since."

"I don't really understand what you're getting at."

"What I'm getting at, Nikita, is that on last Friday evening Yuliya Golova merely overdid it with the strong tea and saw a stranger looming before her, while Pumpianskaya went out that night to get some fresh air, sat herself down on a bench, and died."

"You could be right," said Belotsvetov, "only I stand by my opinion that a new kind of tragedy has transpired. What I mean to say is that the story of Pumpianskaya's fate is revealing when looked at as the latest round in the struggle between good and evil. Some fresh, dark force as yet unknown to man is behind it."

"You're imagining things, Professor," said Chinarikov.

"Maybe I am," answered Belotsvetov humbly. "But what prompts me to imagine these things? The deepest conviction that for quite some time now neither evil nor good in this country have been like good and evil elsewhere — they've been transformed somehow, fed through seventy years of socialist construction. An idea emerges from this . . ."

Chinarikov sighed and attacked the ice with such fervor it was as if he harbored a deep-seated hatred of it.

"An idea based on the historical challenge of our formation, which is to ensure moral construction, to ensure the passage from *Homo sapiens* to *Homo humanus*. And socialism will have a part to play in this not because it is so inclined, but because it has no alternative. In the first place, we've renounced the rule of the sword and other such laws of the jungle as regulators of social order; second, too much in this country is held up by the belief in man's highest potential — though it might be better to say it's all been crumbling lately and not really holding up at all — given that our society is cut loosely, with growing room, like a child's coat . . ."

"That's just the point," said Chinarikov in a sardonic tone, "what's disturbing is that the system's starry-eyed idealism didn't take into account real people!"

"So where's the harm in that? You really don't get it! The gap between the potential of society and the potential of the individual is not a tragedy threatening disaster, but a kind of stimulant that ensures rapid development! Look, in America social potential is a perfect fit for the potential of the individual, and that's why they consider Tolstoy to be a Bolshevik over there . . . In a word, it's like when your boots are too small you get a blister, and when they're too big all you need is an insole. This, by the way, presents a high-priority tactical challenge: the partial liquidation of this gap through the annihilation of primitive evil, of the very evil that originated in animals, which we inherited along with hairiness and fangs. We now find ourselves at a moment in time when this gap must absolutely be liquidated at an accelerated pace, or we might be at risk, at the very least, of having forever to import even pickles.

"What's more, I suspect that the annihilation of the simple most evil is not an epic task, and yet in the whole history of humankind not once has it been undertaken in earnest. It has been undertaken obliquely, of course, through the creation of a new evil, in word, but directly and in earnest — never been done. What factors support my assertion that the liquidation of the simple most evil isn't an epic task? First, not all evil is evil — meaning, we often misinterpret the nature of some acts and take as evil certain public health and safety measures."

"For example?"

"For example, harming a person is wrong, but exposing a scoundrel's true colors is a good deed. Second, a lot could be achieved merely by explaining to people that playing dirty tricks on their fellow man is labor intensive and many times self-injurious, whereas not playing dirty tricks is easy, advantageous, and enjoyable. Third, you've forgotten about the pills for evildoers . . ."

Belotsvetov suddenly fell silent. He'd noticed two passersby and a stray mutt on the opposite side of the alley scrutinizing him and Chinarikov with guarded curiosity. The trio of onlookers had their reasons, by the way. Like it or not, you come to a halt when you encounter a couple of guys armed with yard implements who, instead of clearing ice from the pavement, are waving their arms like madmen and expounding at the top of their lungs on pills for evildoers.

For another five minutes or so after the passersby had moved on, and the mutt had skulked away dejectedly in the direction of the Historical Library, Belotsvetov and Chinarikov worked in silence, but then the conversation resumed.

"But of course the most important point," said Belotsvetov, leaning on his shovel, "is that I'm not calling upon criminals and non-criminals alike to do good. I am suggesting that they simply not commit evil. Let's say some hypothetical scoundrel didn't like my way of thinking and he scribbled a denunciation against me. We have to ask, 'why?' A person has writhed in the throes of authorship, soiled a piece of paper, spent money on an envelope and a stamp — what's the point of it all if I'm already bad off . . . ?"

"Good Lord, what a babe in the woods you are!" exclaimed Chinarikov and, leaning on his implement, he struck the pose of a halberdier. "Even Christ is no match for you, and look at the grief he came to."

"It really is strange: a person is promised, even guaranteed, eternity just so that he doesn't kill, steal, or pervert — in other words, he's offered an absolute benefit and the answer to all questions — and he kills, steals, and perverts all the same. Now, where does that kind of perseverance come from?!"

"It all comes from within, Professor!" said Chinarikov emotionally. "Evil is like matter — endless and eternal."

"If that were true, life would never have advanced beyond the state of primary DNA. The point is, hell is more than likely also eternal life, and so there's not much difference between an eternal that is good and one that is bad. What I'm trying to say is that dealing with the simple most evil — leaving aside madmen for the time being — means proving unequivocally to the ordinary, weak human that not committing evil promises a benefit that's certain and direct. But how is this to be proven if even Christ came to grief? The only thing even somewhat reassuring is that good might be able to ascend the throne on its own. When you think about it, the life of a human being is a microcosm of the history of humankind. Infancy corresponds to the savage stage — it's not for nothing that infants, for example, are so good-natured and spontaneously energetic. Childhood corresponds to antiquity; in this period the human soul cuts its teeth, while humankind becomes conscious of itself as such. By the way, it's very telling that our Petka Golova loves to sing and doesn't think twice about sprinkling magnesium carbonate in someone's tea, or smearing a door handle with muck. Next: the Middle Ages are puberty, with its characteristically absurd prejudices, senseless cruelty, credulity, impatience, and acute sensitivity, all of which proceeds from a love of oneself. Accordingly, youth — that's modern times, with all of its impulses . . . well, and so on . . ."

"Let's say that's so, but what follows from this?"

"A lot of things. First, in his declining years a man becomes innocuous and, therefore, we've no place to hide from the Kingdom of God on Earth — it's inescapable, like the aging of the organism. Second, an evildoer is merely someone who hasn't outgrown adolescence; he's just as absurd and, in essence, as doomed as, say, Nazism, which wouldn't fit these times no matter what the circumstances. Third, to date good has indisputably been the norm and evil the pathology, and a person capable of punching another person in the face must absolutely be isolated from society, like a dangerous lunatic. But mainly what follows from all this is that the mission to further moral construction has fallen to our society. That, you see, is the new Moscow philosophy . . ."

"And the old Moscow philosophy — what's that?"

"The old one — that's Chaadaevism, in the sense that no good has or ever will come out of Russia."

"From everything you've said," said Chinarikov, "what doesn't follow is the most important thing — namely, how does one make it clear as a bell to everyone that the good is advantageous and easy?"

"By God, you're an odd fellow," said Belotsvetov, gesturing oddly with his free hand to corroborate the observation. "If it were that simple all traces of the criminal would've disappeared long ago. We don't need to look hard for an example. Take Adam and Christ — brothers, yet what a difference! What's terrifying is that the raw material is one and the same: flesh encoded with divine potential. No, the point is likely this: if man's becoming is the process of realizing genetic codes through contact with the external world, then it's possible that subhumanity is the result of the deficiency of some crucial information that prevents the code from being fully realized. Just as not all the metal can be smelted from ore if you don't add enough catalyst, or if the oven temperature is set too low, not all the humanity in a person can be cultivated if life has somehow shortchanged him. And out of what? In my opinion, he's been cheated out of limitations, dependencies, a yoke. Because it's possible that, ideally, man is a profoundly limited being, one strictly hemmed in by the laws of virtue. Take you and me, we're limited by the form of the casing we refer to as the body, just like the man of the future will be limited by his essence . . ."

"Listen, Professor!" said Chinarikov crossly. "You came out here to help me, didn't you? So then help me dammit!"

Belotsvetov began obediently to wield the aluminum shovel, but without interrupting his monologue:

"All in all it's a massive misunderstanding that we've set such a high premium on freedom today. We can skip the odd meal but can't do without that freedom. But the reality is, it's a direct indicator of semi-completion, of imperfection — in some respects it's even an anachronism. At one time freedom really was the only path to man's self-realization, the only way out of our animal origins, but today it's an obstacle. Here's proof for you: everything capable of living, that is, in conformity with a purpose, strives to realize itself in its ideal form and is oriented accordingly and, consequently, is constrained."

"Boy, talk about confusing the issue!" said Chinarikov.

"Alright, since you're so thick, I'll give you a concrete example. If, as a viable and rational being, I've set myself the goal of getting married, I'll surely wash myself, dress up as handsomely as I can, and flatter my beloved in every way possible. I'll fawn over her beyond all bounds while at the same time, as a free being, on the way to achieving that goal I can still spend my time arguing with a policeman, stealing twenty rubles from my neighbor, getting drunk, taking a little trip to Arkhangelsk, and throwing myself out of a window. Now do you get it? What I mean is, do you see that freedom of choice overcomes its urgency and becomes a makeweight, the butcher's finger on the scale, as soon as humankind exhausts the possibilities provided by choices based on sound reasoning, as soon as humankind draws on what is *not* subject to choice — that is, the absolute, by virtue of its greater perfection. Under the conditions of the age we live in, this absolute entails a way of life that excludes committing evil against your fellow man. So all that's left is to suggest to a person that he has no choice, that being a real human requires not harming one's fellow man, that to really live means that one does not commit evil, in particular because real life means enjoying the full potential of individual existence and that, in turn, is accessible only to the pure in spirit."

"But what you don't want to take into account," said Chinarikov, "are the time-honored peculiarities of Russian life. Say I decide to get married tomorrow, and on my way to achieving that goal I really do get drunk, steal money from my neighbor, argue with a policeman, take a trip to Arkhangelsk — and get married there instead . . ."

2

Meanwhile, it was business as usual in Apartment 12. Up until lunchtime the course of events was barely perceptible, because Luzhin from Yaroslavl was sleeping on Yuliya Golova's divan, Pyotr was sitting in the kitchen staring out the window, his face stuck to the pane, and Anna Olegovna was working her way through *Tales of the Don*. But sometime after one in the afternoon Lyubov came home from school, and the apartment livened up.

First off, Lyubov fed Pyotr a dish he despised, then she marched him outside for a stroll, then she sat down across from the sleeping Luzhin and said as though to herself:

"It's not nap time, either, this isn't a hospice for the elderly."

The door creaked as it opened, and Mitya shoved his head into the room. For several seconds he looked at Luzhin with disdain, then fixed his eyes on Lyubov and, as though he'd just remembered something, he beckoned her out into the corridor with his index finger.

"Say, sis, do I look like a villain?" asked Mitya disconsolately as soon as Lyubov had closed the door.

"Not to me you don't."

"Well, I am. Sad as it is, I have to admit to being a complete no-good son of a bitch!"

"Why?"

"I can't tell you right now. Just take my word for it: a no-good son of a bitch, that's me. It's interesting how bad it makes you feel to think you're just a mangy skunk. It feels like it's all over for you, like there's nothing to live for . . . like a train's cut off your legs."

"Good grief!" said Lyubov in fright, putting her hand up to her cheek. "What in the world happened? Did you get expelled from school for something?"

"Huh? No . . ."

"Then are you sick? You're white as a sheet."

Mitya looked at Lyubov in the way you look at people you're trying to recognize, but can't.

"Maybe I am sick," he uttered, "it's very possible. There I was, sitting in Chemistry today, thinking, sitting in History, thinking, sitting in English, thinking again . . . !"

"What the heck were you thinking about?"

"That I'm a no-good son of a bitch."

"If you only knew what a no-good . . . well, the one who came from Yaroslavl — you're a saint compared to him. You wouldn't believe the dirty things he's been saying to me!"

Mitya's face changed from naively mournful to angry and lit up with a wicked smile.

The front door slammed, and Chinarikov and Belotsvetov tumbled into the entrance hall. Chinarikov was saying:

". . . Meanwhile, Jerome Lejeune proved long before that the laws of reason correspond somehow to the laws of the universe, while the laws of morality in no way at all. Reason, therefore, developed in accordance with nature, and morality — in spite of it."

"Where did you get that morality is one thing and reason another?" Belotsvetov asked, leading Chinarikov into his room.

"I have my reasons. Let's assume that evil has a multitude of causes of the most empirical origins. They range from the desire for personal gain to the desire to look better than you deserve to in the eyes of your fellow man. But virtue — that is, morality — always emanates from one thing: the soul's rejection of evil . . ."

Whereupon Chinarikov sat down on the sofa and dug into his jeans pocket for a smoke.

"Oh, but no, Vasily, the whole point is that morality and reason are inseparable. It's no coincidence that Adam and Eve realized they were naked as soon as they'd eaten from the Tree of Knowledge. It's no coincidence that only the best, namely, the thinking part of humanity is out of sync with our world . . . In short, everything rational is moral, and everything moral is rational."

"I don't understand what you're getting at," said Chinarikov, and he emitted an enormous cloud of smoke through his nostrils.

"What I'm getting at is that nature's program most certainly took into account the defense of man — a fragile and entirely helpless creature for the first million and a half years of his development — and this defense of man took the form of a writ of safe passage, a certain immune system, if you will, against the onslaught of external misfortunes, against the cruel laws of the dialectic, capable of causing him to wither on the vine. Personal morality came into being through this writ of safe passage, too. It sounds like I'm raving, but this could've been the way it actually worked: it's my rational-moral essence that will never lead me into the company of murderers who could unceremoniously gamble me away in a game of Russian poker."

There was an authoritative knock on the door, and Belotsvetov said, "Come in!"

In came Divisional Inspector Rybkin. He took off his cap, wiped the inside of its crown with his handkerchief, put it onto the back of his head again, and in a voice heavy with fatigue said:

"I'm probably going to have to hand in my resignation soon on account of this apartment of yours . . ."

"One minute, Comrade Rybkin," said Belotsvetov, stopping him, "a few more words and we're at your service. So then, Vasily, virtue is salvation. Being a moral person could mean, even above all else, being someone who is so rational as to fathom that good, or at least not committing evil, is what protects you from misfortune. If you don't give a hoot about the writ of safe passage issued by nature, then you live by the laws of the dialectic — they'll smack you in the face for no reason, you'll get the mumps in old age, and a brick falling from the fifth story will land right on your head. But if you're moral, even passively, then nature will deliver you from all superfluous, unnecessary, undeserved calamities. As well as from some you do deserve."

"And who's the one that got it in the neck yesterday for no good reason?" asked Chinarikov venomously and, emotionally, he crushed his butt in the blue dish on which lay a piece of sugar cube and a dried-out slice of lemon.

"So, what've you got for us, Comrade Rybkin?" asked Belotsvetov, assuming a somewhat dry, business-like expression.

"Well, see, another note from your co-tenant came in. And it's in verse again . . ."

"Never mind that," said Chinarikov. "Especially since there's a much more serious topic to discuss at the moment. What about the Pumpianskaya case, Comrade Rybkin?"

"It's a shady business," said Rybkin.

"It couldn't get any shadier," agreed Belotsvetov despondently. "You don't know the half of it. For example, you don't know that about twenty-four hours after Pumpianskaya's disappearance a mysterious letter addressed to her arrived. It was a death threat demanding the return of some documents, and it was pasted together from letters that had been cut out of *Silver Hoof.* I discovered the cut-up book in Yuliya Golova's room. How do you like that?"

"I don't like it at all," said Rybkin.

"Me neither," admitted Belotsvetov, and he began to pace up and down, as they say. "Therefore, an extremely unusual scenario has unfolded before us: on the anniversary of Collegiate Counselor Pumpiansky's death, his ghost appears in our apartment, terrifying Yuliya Golova . . ."

"Ultimately," interrupted Rybkin, "you'll wind up being denounced as well for your idealistic worldview."

"Right, well," continued Belotsvetov, "so the ghost appeared, terrifying Yuliya Golova. Right after that Pumpianskaya took a Seduxen tablet, made off with a photo of her father — or the ghost made off with its own photo, which it later tore up — and went down to Pokrovsky Boulevard, where she expired from hypothermia shortly afterward. And the next day the letter that was cut out of *Silver Hoof* arrives."

"If we brush aside the ghost hypothesis, then that's just how it was," confirmed Chinarikov.

"Unfortunately, it's not a hypothesis," objected Belotsvetov, "but virtually a clinical fact. Not only did Yuliya smell burnt sulfur, but yesterday Kuznetsova recognized the old man from the photo. What conclusions can be drawn? As ill luck would have it, I can draw only one conclusion: behind all of this lurks some kind of new, dark force — evil, so to speak, of a whole new breed . . . I can feel it, like a rheumatic does foul weather."

Rybkin grew gloomy, and for a length of time he fastened his strangely turgid eyes on the wall. Then he said:

"The main thing is that there is no evidence of a crime — there hasn't even been an incident. There's been nothing other than the death of an old woman, albeit surrounded by some mysterious circumstances."

"You cops, just so long as you don't have to do anything!" said Chinarikov malignantly.

"Listen, get a grip," responded Inspector Rybkin, "control yourself — after all, I'm still on duty!"

Belotsvetov noted:

"And strange as it may seem, I also find it troubling that Petka was sitting in the kitchen on the chamber pot that night, pretending to be browsing through the newspaper."

"It would be much more interesting to find out," said Rybkin, "if Fondervyakin resembles Pumpiansky."

Right away, the faces of Chinarikov and Belotsvetov took on interchangeable expressions of attentiveness.

"How do you mean, resemb– . . . ," uttered Chinarikov, eyes scouring the ceiling. "Of course he resembles him, in the way all baldies resemble one another . . ."

"What do you mean?" asked Belotsvetov. "They're about the same height, too, and even their build is somewhat similar. As a matter of fact, this is the scenario that works for me: it's very possible that it was Fondervyakin whom Yuliya saw in the corridor and then, out of fright, took him to be the old man in the photo. In other words, it's very possible that Fondervyakin was the one who somehow hoodwinked our old lady into dying from hypothermia."

"Maybe we should lean on him?" Chinarikov proposed.

Belotsvetov became interested:

"And how do you plan to lean on him?"

"Simple! The whole gang of us will go to his room right now and demand the skunk own up or else!"

"We could give it a try," said Rybkin.

"I'm warning you, men," announced Belotsvetov, "you'll just end up looking stupid. Especially since the threatening letter originated from Yuliya Golova's family, not from Lev Borisovich."

"Well, let's assume that anyone could've stolen the book from Petka," said Chinarikov. "But the only one resembling the ghost is Lev Borisovich Fondervyakin!"

Suddenly the door to the room opened, and Fondervyakin, looming on the threshold, sadly said:

"Now how on earth could I resemble the ghost. What kind of bull is that?"

Belotsvetov, Chinarikov, Rybkin — all three were unpleasantly surprised.

"And I didn't murder any old lady, either — word of honor,

I didn't murder her! Take my word for it, men — what kind of killer would I make? Why don't you let me own up to another crime instead: do with me what you will, Citizens, but I'm not Fondervyakin . . . !"

"Hmm!" uttered Rybkin. "Who in the world are you then?"

"We've been von der Bakkens from time immemorial. Our surname goes back to the Empress Elizabeth herself — von der Bakken. In forty-one, after the war had already started, Dad slipped a little something to somebody at the registrar's office, and from the von der Bakkens we became the Fondervyakins. But surely you'll agree: the Germans are advancing on Moscow, and here's a family on Petroverigsky Lane whose surname isn't at all in step with the historical moment . . ."

Whereupon the door opened again and, remarkable as it may seem, Alexei Sarantsev peered into the room.

"Oh, here you are!" he said. "I invite you all, please, to attend the funeral lunch . . ."

They didn't grasp what Sarantsev meant at first but, submitting to the welcoming expression on his face, they went out into the corridor and followed him to the kitchen.

3

As should have been expected, Sarantsev and old lady Kuznetsova had only just returned from the Vvedensky Cemetery, where on that Monday Alexandra Sergeyevna Pumpianskaya had been laid to rest, for which occasion they were giving an improvised funeral lunch. A crowd of people had shoved their way into the kitchen: the whole of Apartment 12 plus Dushkin, Superintendent Vostryakova, Pyotr Petrovich Luzhin, who in the simplicity of his heart had joined them, and even two completely unknown men in dark suits, who had found room for themselves by the window.

The funeral lunch turned out to be "incoherent" indeed, as has been said of the same in the St. Petersburg variant of this story. But as it had been there, so here "everything was prepared wonderfully well: the table had even been set quite neatly, the dishes, forks, knives, stemmed glasses, tumblers, cups — all of these things, of course, were an assortment of various styles and various sizes from various tenants, but everything was in its place at the proper time . . ."; well, except the tables were of the kitchen type, albeit covered with tablecloths of various colors. An abundance of democratic goodies, purchased by Sarantsev and Kuznetsova at a delicatessen had been placed on the tables. The tenants, for their part, had added some home-cooked dishes — Kapitonova, for example, had donated a whole dish of aspic. As for the wine, there was only sacramental Cahors. Only a little later, when the lunch had heated up, so to speak, and even thinned out somewhat, did Fondervyakin produce two jars of his fermented apples.

But as for the rest, the similarity between this funeral lunch and that other one was striking, or at least unusual. Zinaida Petrovna Kuznetsova was irritable and quarrelsome, mainly because Pumpianskaya had been buried at the government's expense and in the blink of an eye, so to speak, and from time to time unimaginable orations erupted, and a genuine scandal even broke out: Pyotr Petrovich Luzhin nearly pilfered a bottle of Cahors, which he'd shoved into the pocket of his trousers, but he was exposed by Dushkin and verbally reproached in front of everyone. This unpleasantness was like water off a duck's back for Luzhin, though; he snatched a cabbage turnover and started shoveling it in as if nothing had happened.

That scenes from everyday life separated by a century and a half are so similar invites us to reflect yet again. What if Ecclesiastes was right and there really is nothing new under the sun, and that all is just vanity of vanities, vanity of every ilk, that life rests on and draws its strength from some single, immutable framework that permits only minor deviations from the makeup of its features, and thus it unfolds according to a plan set once and for all and inviolable forever and ever, amen? What if behind this immutability lies the answer to the riddle whereby literature equals the square root of life times talent? It's not impossible that literature was born and continues to exist for the sole reason that billions of lives are copies from a single original, that every life flows out into determined forms — in any case, the part pertaining to events is constructed according to age-old formulas and flows through channels established from time immemorial. It's no coincidence that genuine literary discourse is one that's been purged of its own day and age . . .

What does this hypothesis imply? First, it's possible that in its origin, that is, intrinsically, literature is implicated in the very idea of life, and that if we were to search for the origins of everything in the history of man we would find that no one knows what was in the beginning; it's not impossible that in the beginning was indeed the Word, and that subsequently everything went according to script. Second, it's possible that rather than merely being a crafty reflection of life, literature is the imprinted idea of life itself, with everything that goes along with it — it's no coincidence that the whole of world literature is devoted to the single theme that man is a miracle. In other words, life at its root and literature at its root are one and the same. So it turns out that Francis Bacon was not being in the least bit sly when he claimed that his artistic talent was synonymous with truth. So it turns out that artistic talent is the complicity of the soul in the fundamental laws of life — perhaps more of a one-wombness than complicity. Such being the case, the concepts "life," "talent," and "literature" comprise a trinity, a tri-unity, and not a riddle at all.

A thinking person cannot be dislodged from this position even by the circumstance that instead of the funeral lunch in Apartment 12 beginning with the words, "That cuckoo is to blame for everything. You know who I'm talking about: her, her!" it began with Zinaida Petrovna Kuznetsova taking a few steps toward the middle of the kitchen and weepily proclaiming:

"Come, Comrades, let us commemorate, according to Russian custom, the newly departed servant of God, Alexandra . . ."

Everyone raised their glasses, became stock-still, took a deep breath, took a drink, and took another deep breath. Rybkin was the only one who held up his glass and put it back in its place without having touched a drop.

"What about you, then, Comrade Inspector?" Fondervyakin asked him with phony concern.

"What an odd question . . . ," said Rybkin. "I'm on duty, after all . . ."

"You're a man of sound character," Belotsvetov commended him, "a character that is acutely Continental, so to speak."

"On duty — big deal!" Superintendent Vostryakova joined in. "For all intents and purposes I'm on duty, too, but I didn't let the gang down. As the saying goes, duty may be duty, but folk customs are sacred."

"If I understand the idea correctly," said Alexei Sarantsev crossly, "funeral lunches were invented for the purpose of remembering the deceased . . . Although, in all honesty, I don't remember the deceased at all."

"She was a nice old woman, what else is there to say . . . ," announced Yuliya Golova. "Educated, good-hearted, thrifty, and healthy as a horse. If not for these communal conditions she would definitely have outlived us all."

"And what, in fact, do communal conditions have to do with anything?" objected Anna Olegovna Kapitonova. "We've always lived in perfect harmony in our apartment. Before the war, during the war, after the war, right up to the unmasking of the cult of personality, and when everything went willy-nilly."

"Nevertheless, we did Alexandra Sergeyevna in just the same. And what did we do her in for? Her little room!" said Belotsvetov.

Inspector Rybkin knitted his brows and stated:

"This, Citizens, has yet to be proven."

"We may even have to abandon this scenario altogether," said Belotsvetov looking pensively at the floor. "At first we did actually think we'd done Alexandra Sergeyevna in solely because of her little room, but yesterday we received quite the intriguing missive . . ."

"Now, this is interesting!" said Genrikh Valenchik, paling.

"Interesting isn't the word for it," continued Belotsvetov. "If you like, I'll read yesterday's letter out to you — perhaps in the presence of such a gathering of interested parties its meaning will be somewhat clarified. Vasily, go and fetch the letter, please. I put it under the bust of Apukhtin in your room."

Chinarikov left to fetch the letter, while Dushkin took advantage of the pause to propose they each have another nip. Sarantsev poured what was left of the wine, Kuznetsova chanted "Memory Eternal," and everybody knocked back their drinks.

After a minute, Chinarikov returned. He came right up close to Belotsvetov and said in an undertone:

"You know, the strangest thing has happened: somebody's stolen the portrait of Hemingway from my room. I happened to look at the wall just now, as if someone had nudged me to, and instead of the portrait I saw an empty space . . . !"

Belotsvetov looked at Chinarikov in bewilderment, shrugged his shoulders, then cleared his throat and began loudly to read the text.

"That, Comrades, is the pickle we're in," he said in conclusion. "Any ideas?"

In the kitchen there settled the type of silence we call gravelike. Finally, Alexei Sarantsev said:

"As for me, I can't make heads or tails of it, as the saying goes!"

"I didn't understand anything either," admitted Anna Olegovna, fixing her violet ringlets.

Fondervyakin took a step forward and solemnly declared:

"I warned way back when that this business was evil! I said then that this reeked of sabotage by enemy agents!"

"Calm down, Lev Borisovich," said Belotsvetov. "Enemy agents don't have anything to do with this. This letter story smells more like slander. To tell you the truth, it's only just occurred to me that perhaps someone wanted to defame our old lady. What's relevant is that the note is composed of letters that have been cut out of *Silver Hoof*, and I discovered just such a book, mangled through and through, in Yuliya Golova's room . . ."

At these words Belotsvetov looked inquiringly at Yuliya Golova, and she met his glance serenely, even impudently.

Mitya Nachalov frowned and said:

"So, Nikita Ivanovich, it seems you've been rummaging through other people's belongings! Is this the deed you promised?"

"Meaning what?" Belotsvetov asked in miscomprehension.

"Not long ago you promised me a certain deed would prove that not all adults were scoundrels, remember?"

"Yes, I did promise you, didn't I . . . ," Belotsvetov uttered, becoming confused and falling silent.

In the meantime, the two jars of Fondervyakin's preserved apples appeared — to which Rybkin reacted with condescension for some reason — and the conversation became much more chaotic and heated.

Addressing Genrikh Valenchik, Chinarikov said:

"Listen, mister writer, you wouldn't happen to be the one who composed the poison-pen letter, would you? The word is you're the big specialist around here in literary denunciations."

"Vera, go away," ordered Genrikh and, having turned to face Chinarikov, said: "Go ahead and talk, Vasily, but watch what you say! I don't write anonymous poison-pen letters. I prefer to use the tools of literary discourse to unmask life. So if you don't understand a goddamn thing about such matters, keep your big nose out of them!"

"Exactly!" piped in Vera from the corridor.

"Of course, there might be some things I don't fully understand," admitted Chinarikov, "but all the same, you'd better choose your words more carefully."

"You'll come to blows!" Yuliya Golova admonished them. "And

there just happens to be someone here who can set you up on bread and water in no time flat."

"You can write till the cows come home, boys, but the one moving into the old lady's room is me," said Dushkin.

"See this?" exclaimed Fondervyakin, giving him the finger.

"Don't you make obscene gestures at me," uttered Dushkin, "go ahead and ask Vostryakova whom she intends to move in there."

"The only thing I can say," responded Vostryakova, "is that we're in no position these days to spread our personnel too thin."

Belotsvetov poked Chinarikov in the side and in a hushed voice muttered:

"Don't you think that character over there," he motioned with his head in the direction of one of the strangers in dark suits huddled by the window, "bears a striking resemblance to our venerable ghost?"

"You know, you might be on to something," Chinarikov whispered back. "Only judging from his appearance this guy is sixty years old max, not a hundred and eighteen."

"But here's the thing: it doesn't need to have been old man Pumpiansky himself who showed up here in the guise of old man Pumpiansky; it could have been his son, Georgy Sergeyevich, who allegedly was killed in the battle for Moscow . . ."

"Hmm . . . ," pondered Chinarikov, "that's a thought . . ."

Meanwhile, the feud between Dushkin and Fondervyakin had already reached that critical stage when one can do little more than arm oneself with whatever objects are immediately at hand and proceed directly into a brawl. We can only assume a brawl would indeed have ensued if not for District Inspector Rybkin.

"Come now, Citizens," said he, "control yourselves. Show some restraint, you're not in a beer hall . . ."

"They're mad as all hell!" added Anna Olegovna, tossing her violet ringlets indignantly. "They're liable to bash each other's heads in over a lousy pawn!"

"If only it were over a pawn!" Fondervyakin corrected her. "You might say what's at stake here is a matter of life and death — I mean, the augmentation of living space!"

"Now that's another story," agreed Anna Olegovna, either in earnest or ironically. "You really could bash someone's head in over a few extra square meters."

"Come now, let's finally decide this question like human beings, on democratic grounds," Genrikh implored. "For four days we haven't been able to divvy up among us ten miserable square meters! What's more, all peaceful initiatives are being openly sabotaged! This isn't an apartment, it's a mob of renegades — and I say this in all honesty!"

"Begging your magnanimous pardon, but the one moving into the little room is me!" sneered Dushkin.

"Comrade Rybkin," complained Fondervyakin, "crack down on this insolent jerk already . . ."

Rybkin held his tongue. He took his cap off his head, wiped the inside of its crown with his handkerchief, stuck it on the back of his head again, and his eyes seemed to indicate that he was just about to say something interesting — but he held his tongue.

"Or else I can't be held responsible for my actions," continued Fondervyakin. "Look," he said, "I'll take this roaster," pointing at Kapitonova's roaster with his head, "and flat out let this snake have it!"

Belotsvetov rubbed his face, sized up the gathering, and said:

"Listening to you, dear fellow countrymen, makes my hair stand on end. We together and each of us individually happen to have the honor of belonging to a people to whom, by virtue of its somewhat peculiar historical path, the mission of moral construction has fallen. It is your lot, my dearest contemporaries, my brothers and sisters by blood, to answer before the world and history for the further spiritual evolution of man, but hearing you carry on makes me want to hang myself . . ."

"What the hell kind of bunk is that?" asked Luzhin from Yaroslavl with a hint of indignation.

Nobody answered him.

The gathering had grown altogether somber, and then it began quietly to disperse. When there was barely anyone left in the kitchen, Belotsvetov walked up to Alexei Sarantsev and asked:

"Listen, who were those guys with you?"

"What guys?" asked Sarantsev in surprise.

"The two in the dark suits, with the gloomy mugs — relations by any chance?"

"What are you talking about, old man? Some relations!" replied Sarantsev. "One is the undertaker and the other drives the whatsit . . . the hearse."

"Hmm!" responded Belotsvetov. "That's interesting, and what on earth were they doing at the funeral lunch?"

"How should I know?! Maybe they got tired of their woeful business, or maybe they just felt like having a snack . . ."

"It's a wonder you didn't invite the gravediggers as well," observed Chinarikov.

After Sarantsev left, only Chinarikov and Belotsvetov remained in the kitchen, along with Pyotr Golova who, as was his wont, was sitting on the stool swinging his legs. A kind of gleefully wicked smile lit up his face.

"Well, what do you say, Pyotr?" asked Chinarikov, addressing the boy idly and winking pensively.

"Here's what I say," replied Pyotr, "you don't know anything, but I do . . ."

Chinarikov and Belotsvetov pricked up their ears and nervously fixed their gazes upon Pyotr, who was silent and smiling mockingly.

"Interesting. I wonder, what is it you know?" asked Belotsvetov.

"Come on, now, talk — don't drag it out!"

Just to be nasty, Pyotr held out a little longer before reporting:

"I know who was in the bathroom that night."

"Who?" exclaimed Chinarikov and Belotsvetov.

"Mitka Nachalov, that's who!"

"Why the heck didn't you say so before?!" asked Chinarikov with annoyance.

"I just didn't feel like it, that's all."

"And now you feel like it?"

"Now I feel like it."

"What a piece of work!" said Belotsvetov.

"I also know who ruined the book about the silver hoof. Lyubka, the dummy, she ruined my book."

"That's the younger generation for you!" Chinarikov was outraged. "Selling out your own sister, just like that!"

"Listen, Vasily," said Belotsvetov. "We need to go and sort things out with our golden youth. Seeing as you and I have taken this business upon ourselves, we've got to see it through to the victorious end."

"You said it!"

Pyotr Petrovich Luzhin popped into the kitchen.

"Who was calling me?" he asked belligerently. "Who needs to clap eyes on me before bed?"

Belotsvetov shrugged his shoulders in reply and mutely led Chinarikov into the corridor. But no sooner had they gone around the bend connecting the kitchen to the living area, than an uncanny sight was revealed to them: not far from the front door dimly glowed the ghost of Ernest Hemingway.

4

The corridor reeked of something singed. For about half a minute the two friends stood there flaring their nostrils and maintaining an anxious silence. The first to come to his senses was Chinarikov, as indeed is customary for a card-carrying materialist. Resolute and purposeful, he stepped toward the ghost, got almost as far as the door to the landing, turned to the right, drew up close to the antique mirror, felt it with his hand for some reason, and gaily shouted:

"Don't be a wimp and get over here!"

Belotsvetov obeyed the summons and deliberately shoved his hands into his pants' pockets.

"Look, you pathetic idealist! This is no ghost, it's nothing but a projection of the Ernest Hemingway photo someone made off with today."

Indeed, upon closer examination Hemingway's ghost didn't look like a ghost at all. The image was flat, and in addition a few fine scratches on the background as well as a fingerprint had been reproduced.

"Mitka's in the bathroom again," they suddenly heard behind them, and Chinarikov and Belotsvetov turned around. In the middle of the entrance hall stood Pyotr Golova, chewing malignantly on his thumbnail, while a blinding white light streamed from the transom window over the bathroom door.

"Now I get it!" said Chinarikov with a bitter smile, and he made for the bathroom.

He pounded the door with his fist and listened — silence.

"Dmitry, is that you ensconced in there?" shouted Chinarikov through the chink between the door and the jamb.

"Well, I . . . ," responded Mitya reluctantly, and that very second the blinding white light stopped streaming through the transom window over the door.

"What do you think you're doing, you rogue — putting on a show for us, eh?!"

"Why's this old goat from Yaroslavl chasing after Lyubov? Aren't there enough Yaroslavlian little heifers for him, or what . . . ?"

"So you wanted to scare the visitor?"

"Well of course!" came from behind the door. "Or else you get all kinds showing up here from the provinces, and just to get a Moscow residence permit they start hitting on our naive youth . . . !"

Flaring his nostrils fiercely, Chinarikov said:

"Do you realize, you La Manchian son of a bitch, that you and that idiotic ghost of yours did in Alexandra Pumpianskaya?! When she saw her late father, she must've immediately taken the backstairs right out of the building! And to the very bench where she later expired from hypothermia! Do you understand this or not?!"

"I do . . . ," answered Mitya quietly.

"Does that mean you were also the one who stole old man Pumpiansky's photograph?" Belotsvetov asked him.

"I was the one who stole the photograph, and the one who threw it out, to destroy the only evidence, and the one who wrote the letter about the documents, as a diversion, and the one who came up with the way to project the ghost, too. I wanted to write something scary for the old woman in Latin letters as well, but then I thought that would be too much."

"Listen! You'd better come out of that bathroom," demanded Chinarikov, "this seems like an idiotic way to have a conversation."

"Not on your life!" answered Mitya, his voice nervously high-pitched.

Meanwhile, the scene by the bathroom door had already begun to attract unwanted attention: Luzhin from Yaroslavl was on the point of trying to edge his way into the conversation; Fondervyakin was leaning out of his room; Vera Valenchik was peering out at the commotion. Yet Chinarikov calmed all of them down and sent them away.

"There's only one thing I can't understand," said Belotsvetov. "I mean, it's impossible to project an image onto a mirrored surface, but you managed it, Dmitry, you devil!"

"It's not complicated at all," Mitya informed him. "A system of compact lenses, an especially strong source of light, plus I smeared the mirror with gelatin, and what you get is a real ghost — if you look at it from a distance, of course."

"And it stinks a little when you're doing it, right?"

"It does, a little. Yes . . . it was also me who called from a pay phone to lure the old lady out of her room and steal the old man's photo from her."

"Don't lie!" suddenly boomed Lyubov's voice, and Chinarikov and Belotsvetov turned their heads. "Don't lie — I was the one who phoned . . ."

"Actually" said Mitya from behind the door, "I really only wanted to test my apparatus for projecting ghosts on our old woman. How was I supposed to know she'd get so frightened she'd run out and die for no good reason . . ."

"So . . . ," Chinarikov pronounced, lowering his chin onto his chest and looking dismally at the floor. "Well, how do the both of you intend to live from this point on? The question is, how do the both of you intend to live with yourselves after what you've caused, you degenerates?"

"I don't know . . . ," answered Mitya candidly, then added after a short pause: "Believe it or not, I'm worried sick. I've been out of my mind with anxiety for two days now. Ever since it hit home that the old lady died because of me, I've been out of my mind with anxiety. Maybe it's best if they go ahead and lock me up."

"Oh they'll lock you up alright!" Chinarikov assured him. "They'll definitely lock you up, you can count on it!"

"Mit, oh Mit!" said Lyubov, pressing her face against the bathroom door. "Don't worry about them locking you up. I'll follow you wherever they send you. I'll make my home in a shack by the prison and live there just so you'll know you're not alone in your anguish."

"What about your studies?" asked Mitya in an adult sort of way.

"Well, they must have schools there to educate the jailers.

You'll work in the mines while I go to school in the morning, and in the evening I'll bring you parcels."

"Even if they don't lock me up," said Mitya pensively, "I'll volunteer for unskilled labor up in the far north and live in a way that will serve as a kind of rightful punishment for myself. Especially because I'm not afraid of it — in fact, I demand it, because I have the right to punishment in the same way the sick have the right to treatment and care."

Belotsvetov said:

"Rest assured, either way you slice it what awaits you isn't a normal life at all, but one of continual rightful punishment. Or maybe wrongful, I don't know."

Chinarikov put his face against the door and said:

"Alright, enough horsing around. Come on, get out of there! Or else you'll do something stupid and then Nikita and I will blame ourselves for the rest of our lives."

"I'm not coming out, Vas," responded Dmitry, "so don't even suggest it. Think of it as though I've sentenced myself to solitary confinement until things get sorted out."

"Oh go to hell then!" said Chinarikov. "Go ahead and sit in there to your heart's content, but we're leaving."

With these words Chinarikov went to the kitchen, Pyotr trudged along right behind him, Belotsvetov went to his place, while Lyubov hunkered down by the bathroom door, propping her head up on her elbow.

It was around eleven o'clock at night. Anna Olegovna had long since gone to sleep behind the screen in her room; having settled Luzhin down to bed on the floor, Yuliya Golova was sitting in front of the mirror preparing her overnight beauty mask; Fondervyakin tossed and turned as sleep evaded him; Vera Valenchik was crocheting; Genrikh, pen in hand, continued to sit staring through the wall, just as he'd been doing for the past hour.

Belotsvetov paced back and forth from the window to the door in his room for some time, mulling over the peculiarities of present-day morality in light of Mitya's behavior. For some reason he couldn't think, couldn't conjecture. Belotsvetov walked out of his room into the corridor, went up to the antique mirror and touched it with his hand. Then he went to the kitchen and, bending down along the way, patted Lyubov on the head.

Though no light was on in the kitchen, the moon, high in the sky, gave off enough illumination for Belotsvetov at once to see Vasily Chinarikov sitting by the window with Pyotr nestled in his lap. Both were looking at the moon, heads thrown slightly back, and softly singing, ". . . In his land Allah is behind every rock / But who will protect me, an orphan . . . ," and Pyotr was singing terribly off-key in keeping with his young years.

Belotsvetov went back to the bathroom, knocked on the door, and said:

"Have a conscience, Dmitry! It's nighttime, and Lyuba's sitting here beside the door like a dog because of you!"

"Let her go to bed," responded Mitya, "I'm not stopping her."

"You're a smart ass, I'll give you that much! Lyuba's behaving just like Sonya Marmeladova, and you're scoffing at her, you son of a bitch!"

"Who the hell's Sonya Marmeladova?" asked Mitya, angry and confused.

"Oh, for crying out loud!" said Belotsvetov. "You mean you've never read *Crime and Punishment*?"

"Well, no, I haven't . . . What am I supposed to do about it now — hang myself?!"

"You don't have to hang yourself, but you ought to read *Crime and Punishment*."

Mitya said nothing in reply. Belotsvetov stood deep in thought opposite the bathroom door a little longer, and with a slow, lugubrious step he went back to his room. He sat down at the table, moved aside an end crust of rye bread and an eggshell with his elbow, picked up a pen, found a scrap of paper, and began to jot down the thoughts Mitya had evoked, in order not to forget to discuss them with Chinarikov the next day. Distilled from these ruminations was the idea that in the process of humankind's moral development, literature had even been assigned a genetic significance of sorts, because literature was humankind's spiritual experience in concentrated form, and therefore it was the most essential supplement to the rational being's genetic code, that exclusive of literature a person could not fully achieve his potential as such. Certain things were handed down from generation to generation in the blood of our forebears, but other things only by means of books. It thus followed that people were obliged to live their lives circumspectly, keeping literature closely in mind as their measure, like Christians and the Lord's Prayer.

TRANSLATOR'S NOTE

Vyacheslav Pyetsukh's appearance on the Russian literary scene coincided with glasnost, a period in Soviet history of exceptional artistic freedom whose literary texts vary greatly in terms of style, theme, and even ideological perspective. Satire is a given in the late-Soviet narrative. In *The New Moscow Philosophy*, Pyetsukh's satire is double-edged in that he lampoons not only the cynical late-Soviet human condition, but also the promises of glasnost on the threshold of a new era that stirs up complex emotions and attitudes in his characters, ranging from anticipation of the future to nostalgia for the past, and even for the present, the late-Soviet status quo.

As a text of glasnost, *The New Moscow Philosophy* first attracted me with its parody of Dostoevsky's *Crime and Punishment*, and the *nature* of this parody made it even more compelling in that it differed substantially from what was "typical" in the late- and anti-Soviet narratives I had been researching. Parody is a complex mode of discourse with diverse goals, and theoretical positions vary on how it should be defined. On its simplest, most evident and aggressive level, parody usually involves the outright subversion, or the negation, of its target — say, of the officially sanctioned paradigm of Socialist Realism. But at its most subtle and neutral, parody hinges on the tension evoked by the irony the reader perceives in the relationship between the work and its target as the former is superimposed over the latter. Parody of this sort often merely underscores "critical distance." In fact, the target text need not be the object of criticism, in which case the result is discourse bordering on *self*-parody as tribute is paid to the target often at the parody's *own* expense.[1] *The New Moscow Philosophy* should be viewed within this context. Rather than subvert his target text, Pyetsukh is overtly reverential toward it at the expense of his own narrative, which is not an equivalent of *Crime and Punishment* but a watered-down, late-Soviet variant, a meta-literary, nostalgic homage to Dostoevsky's classic and the classical Russian literary tradition as a symbiosis of literature and life.

Rich, complex, and challenging for reader and translator alike, the novel appeared in French, German, Italian, and Spanish translations between 1990 and 1992, but until now has been overlooked in a complete English translation.[2] Perhaps the more scintillating "cruel" and "dark" prose of glasnost seemed more urgent at the time, or perhaps it was because of the very complexities that make it such an interesting, humorous, and thought-provoking read.

One of the many challenges I encountered was finding the proper tone in translation for a savvy narrator who impassively, yet intrusively, and not without a good deal of irony and humor,

1. See Linda Hutcheon, *Theory of Parody* (New York: Methuen, 1985) and "Modern Parody and Bakhtin" in *Rethinking Bakhtin: Extensions and Challenges*, eds. Gary Saul Morson and Caryl Emerson (Evanston: Northwestern UP, 1989).
2. One section, however, did appear in English: "Part II: Saturday," trans. David Gillespie, in *Soviet Literature* (1990: 1) 86–107.

considers the nature of the literary text, the intricate relationship between literature and life, and the role of the Russian literary narrative — glasnost prose included — in forming the psyche of the average Russian reader. He does so in a seamless mix of registers, ranging from the formal to the casual and richly idiomatic. Equally challenging was the related problem of creating natural-sounding dialogue between characters ranging in age from six to sixty-plus, in discussions ranging from the official and the philosophical to the prosaic, from the heated to the sullen, from the impassioned to the indignant. What I found appealing about the novel both as reader and translator is its utter absence of pretentiousness despite the elevated topics it examines and presents for our consideration. It's no wonder, then, that Pyetsukh is a major figure on the Russian literary stage, or that his fiction and non-fiction, early and current, is so popular among the Russians who, like himself, see a sense of irony and humor as the two most important constants in life.

I am indebted to Prof. Lyudmila Parts of McGill University's Department of Russian for her invaluable help, guidance, and moral support through every stage of this project, literally from start to finish. Heartfelt thanks go to Prof. Laura Beraha, also of McGill's Russian department, for steering me through some tricky parts of Pyetsukh's text. Thanks also to Marina Swoboda and to those on SEELANGS who replied to my queries. I am grateful to Vyacheslav Pyetsukh himself for being so gracious and accommodating, and to Howard Sidenberg of Twisted Spoon Press for believing in this project. Last but never least, I thank my husband Nory, as always.

I dedicate this translation to my brother Rich.

NOTES

p. 11   *some school teacher from Saratov:* a reference to Nikolai
         Chernyshevsky (1828–1889), literary critic and leader of the
         Russian radical intelligentsia in the 1860s, author of the utopian-
         utilitarian novel *What Is to be Done?* (1863).

p. 12   *"In the beginning of July":* opening passage from Fyodor
         Dostoevsky's *Crime and Punishment* (1866). Here as elsewhere
         Dostoevsky polemicizes with Chernyshevsky.

p. 12   *Izmailovsky Imperial Guards Regiment:* a military regiment formed
         in 1730, it gave its name to a St. Petersburg suburb (*Izmailovsky polk*).

p. 13   *Captain Lebyadkin:* a character in Dostoevsky's *The Devils* (1872).

p. 13   *"Singlethought":* Nikolai Leskov's (1831–95) story "Odnodum"
         (1879, also translated as "One Track Mind").

p. 14   *"She cried out, though very weakly":* *Crime and Punishment*, part I,
         chap. VII, the final throes of Alyona Ivanovna, the old money-
         lender murdered by Raskolnikov.

p. 18   *Kolyma hydroelectric plant:* Built in the 1970s at Kolyma, Siberia,
         the site of the Soviet Union's most notorious gulag.

p. 20   *Red Field: Krasnaia niva*, illustrated weekly sociopolitical journal of literature and the arts published from 1923 to 1931.

p. 21   *the new orthography:* spelling reform introduced by the new Soviet government in 1918. To use the old spelling was a form of political protest.

p. 21   *Tsar Nicholas the Bloody:* Tsar Nicholas II, so named for Bloody Sunday, signalling the start of the failed revolution of 1905.

p. 22   *vologodsky collar:* intricately embroidered lace around the neckline, often midway down the front of a dress or blouse.

p. 28   *Evergreen Game:* a famous chess match between Adolf Anderssen and Jean Dufesne in 1852.

p. 31   *papirosa:* the Belomorkanal brand of cigarette that was 2/3 hollow cardboard tube in lieu of a filter and 1/3 paper filled with tobacco. Popular during the Soviet era because they were so cheap.

p. 34   *Armenian Lane:* historically the center of the Moscow Armenian community.

p. 42   *Teffi:* Nadezhda Teffi (1872-1952), popular prose writer, dramatist, humorist, and poet.

p. 45   *"By the way, do you believe in ghosts?":* Crime and Punishment, part IV, chap. I, an exchange between Raskolnikov and Svidrigailov about the latter's late wife, Marfa Petrovna.

p. 52   *Nikolai Uspensky:* (1837–89) Russian writer turned alcoholic street buffoon and storyteller. Once admired by Chernyshevsky for his unflattering, realistic portrayals of the Russian peasantry.

p. 53   *" 'My Dear Sir,' he began almost solemnly":* Crime and Punishment, part I, chap. II, from Marmeladov's monologue.

p. 54   *"Why, moonshine will get you almost as much time in the clink today as high treason!"*: a reference to Gorbachev's anti-alcohol campaign of the mid-1980s.

p. 55   *Zagorsk:* location of the famous Trinity Monastery of St. Sergius, the religious center of Russian Orthodoxy and a place of pilgrimage. Changed back to its original name, Sergiyev Posad, in 1991.

p. 55   *KVN:* the first domestic Russian mass-produced black-and-white TV set, sold from 1949 to 1960.

p. 57   *the Arbat:* historic center of Moscow, once the bohemian quarter.

p. 61   *NEP:* the New Economic Policy (1921–28) instated by Lenin following the Civil War to prevent total economic collapse after the radical centralization of War Communism (1918–21).

p. 62   *Grushnitsky:* a character in Mikhail Lermontov's *A Hero of Our Time* (1840). A parody of the romantic hero, Grushnitsky is a poseur who is killed in a duel by Lermontov's cynical alter-ago, Pechorin.

p. 63   *Kozelsk:* a town in western Russia, close to the Optina Hermitage (*Optina pustyn*), a monastery for men said to have been the most important spiritual center of the Russian Orthodox Church in the 19th century.

p. 69   *"Farewell, unwashed Russia"*: the opening lines of a poem by Mikhail Lermontov, written on the occasion of his second (and last) exile from Russia to the Caucasus (1840 or 1841).

p. 70   *"Why are you breaking chairs"*: a reference to Nikolai Gogol's play *The Inspector General* (1836).

p. 70   *"But why in the world break chairs"*: *Crime and Punishment*, part III, chap. V; Porfiry Petrovich is the criminal investigator.

p. 71   *Apukhtin:* Alexei Nikolaevich (1840–93), poet, prose writer, and critic, whose lyrical verse was set to music by Tchaikovsky.

p. 75   *the student Ivanov's murder:* Ivanov was murdered in 1869 by the anarchist and nihilist Sergei Nechayev, who appears in *The Devils* as Pyotr Stepanovich Verkhovensky; Shatov represents Ivanov.

p. 91   *the blood spilled at Kandahar:* referring to the Soviet-Afghan War, 1979–89.

p. 91   *Minister of War Milyutin:* a nobleman by birth, renowned for his sweeping reforms of the Russian military in the 19th century.

p. 95   *Ivan Ivanovich Dushkin:* historically, a Soviet hero of WWII. In general usage, "Ivan Ivanovich" translates as "your average Joe."

p. 97   *pelmeni:* a traditional Siberian dumpling filled with meat.

p. 102   *Pierre Bezukhov:* a young idealist and central character in Tolstoy's *War and Peace* (1865-1869).

p. 103   *Yudushka Golovlevs:* from Saltykov-Shchedrin's satirical novel *The Golovlev Family* (1875–80). The main character, Porfiry Golovlev, is nicknamed Yudushka (Little Judas). Depicted as a liar, hypocrite, and tyrant, he uses deceit to usurp ownership of the family estate.

p. 105   *"the stairway was very narrow":* Crime and Punishment, part II, chap. I, as is the passage that follows.

p. 106   *Merezhkovsky-Gippius-Filosofov triangle:* a famous love triangle during Russia's literary Silver Age involving the decadent poet Dmitry Sergeyevich Merezhkovsky (1865–1941), his wife Zinaida Gippius (1869–1945), and collaborator Dmitry Filosofov (1872–1940).

p. 106   *Blok-Mendeleyeva-Bely triangle:* symbolist poet Alexander Blok (1880–1921), his wife Lyubov Dmitriyevna Mendeleyeva, and fellow symbolist writer Andrei Bely (1880–1934), author of the novel *Petersburg* (1916).

p. 107   *Chernyshevsky, Olga Sokratovna, and all of Saratov:* Chernyshevsky's wife, Olga, was famous in Saratov for her promiscuity.

p. 113   *October holidays:* the anniversary of the October (Bolshevik) Revolution in 1917.

p. 113   *Seduxen:* the sedative Diazepam (Valium).

p. 116   *wet job:* (or "wet work") literal translation of the Russian *mokroye delo,* a KGB euphemism for an assassination.

p. 117   *Academician Vernadsky:* Vladimir Ivanovich (1863–1945), noted Russian geochemist and mineralogist who made important contributions to the understanding of the biosphere.

p. 121   *Burda:* a fashion magazine with sewing patterns for the clothing featured in each issue.

p. 125   *glasnost:* initiated in 1985, Mikhail Gorbachev's policy calling for openness, greater access to information, and relaxation of censorship in the Soviet Union to foster governmental transparency.

p. 127   *Silver Hoof:* a Russian fairy tale about a magical deer whose hooves leave behind precious stones wherever they strike.

p. 130   *War Communism:* the economic and political system put in place during the Russian Civil War (1918–21) that included the radical centralization and nationalization of Russia's resources in addition to various other drastic measures implemented by the Bolsheviks to fuel the Red Army.

p. 132   *Vysotsky:* Vladimir Semyonovich (1938–80), a hugely popular, covertly anti-Soviet balladeer, poet, songwriter, and actor.

p. 139   *the woes of wit:* referring to the play *The Woes of Wit*, a popular satirical comedy by Alexander Sergeyevich Griboedov (1795–1829).

p. 141   *Pyotr Petrovich Luzhin:* a villain in *Crime and Punishment*, betrothed to Raskolnikov's sister, Dunya, who hopes the marriage will ensure financial security for her mother and brother.

p. 149   *Chaadaevism:* the view of Russian philosopher Pyotr Yakovlevich Chaadaev (1794–1856) that nothing good had come from Russia, or ever would unless it changed course and aligned itself with Western thought.

p. 159   *"everything was prepared wonderfully well":* Crime and Punishment, part V, chap. II, referring to the table set for Marmeladov's funeral lunch.

p. 161   *"That cuckoo is to blame for everything":* Crime and Punishment, part V, chap. II, uttered by Marmeladov's destitute widow, Katerina Ivanovna, about the landlady at his funeral lunch.

ABOUT THE AUTHOR

Vyacheslav Alekseyevich Pyetsukh was born in Moscow in 1946. First published in 1978, he became a member of the Russian PEN Center after the collapse of the Soviet Union in 1991 and served as editor-in-chief of one of the major literary journals, *Druzhba narodov*, from 1993 to 1995. He has published fifteen collected editions of his work, and both his essays and short stories appear regularly in the leading Russian journals. In English, his work has appeared in *The Penguin Book of New Russian Writing*, *Absinthe*, *Antioch Review*, *St. Petersburg Review*, and *Words without Borders*. His story "Me and the Sea" was awarded the 1999 Emily Clark Balch Prize of the *Virginia Quarterly Review*. Pyetsukh has been honored with many of Russia's most pretigious awards: the Pushkin Prize in 2007; the National Ecological Award in 2009, given by the Vernadsky Foundation, for his "creative contribution" to enlightening on environmental issues in Russia; the 2010 Triumph Award for excellence in the arts and literature. He and his wife Irina, an art dealer specializing in avant-garde painting, divide their time between Moscow and a village in the Tverskaya region.

ABOUT THE TRANSLATOR

Krystyna Anna Steiger was born and raised in Toronto. A recipient of numerous awards and fellowships, she received her Ph.D in Russian Literature from McGill University, in Montreal, where she currently resides with her husband, the painter Nory Marc Steiger. She currently works as a freelance literary translator.

The New Moscow Philosophy by Vyacheslav Pyetsukh
is translated by Krystyna Steiger from the original Russian
"Novaia moskovskaia filosofiia," *Novyi mir* 1 (1989): 54-125.

An earlier version of "Friday" appeared in *St. Petersburg Review*

Cover and section image by Dan Mayer
Design by Jed Slast
Set in Janson

FIRST EDITION

Published in 2011 by
Twisted Spoon Press
P.O. Box 21 – Preslova 12
150 21 Prague 5
Czech Republic
www.twistedspoon.com

Printed and bound in the Czech Republic by PB Tisk

Distributed to the trade by
CENTRAL BOOKS
99 Wallis Road
London, E9 5LN
United Kingdom
www.centralbooks.com

SCB DISTRIBUTORS
15608 South New Century Drive
Gardena, CA 90248-2129
USA
www.scbdistributors.com